Catharine Collingridge

NO ADMITTANCE AFTER DARK

LAURENCE GREEN

Laurence Green (signature)

Durrant Arms

see p. 157 !

MOORHEN PUBLISHING

First published in Great Britain in 2012 by
Moorhen Publishing
1 Hazelwood Close, Windmill Hill, Brixham, Devon, TQ5 9SE
www.moorhenpublishing.co.uk

ISBN   978-1-905856-16-9

Cover design by Tammie Doe
using an original drawing by Catharine Collingridge
Printed and bound in Great Britain by
SRP Limited, Exeter, Devon

Dedication

This book is dedicated to my dear wife
Kathi

Contents

Tiddly Suits in Guz

Being a Janner born and bred I always enjoyed a run ashore when our ship, H.M.S. Eclipse, returned to Devonport. His Majesty's Royal Navy was my life and my career, but dry land pulled me home from time to time.

My ship brought me home to a Plymouth devastated by the Luftwaffe. It was late May of 1941; Drake Circus and most of the centre of town lay in ruins. The buses and cabs threaded their slow way through mounds of rubble down streets changed beyond all recognition. Charles Church raised high walls and empty windows to a grey sky. St Andrew's had fared not much better, but life went on despite our cruel loss.

Union Street resembled a bloody jaw from which several teeth had been violently bashed. It stretched from the city centre out towards the dockyard and Devonport. Rubble still mounded the pavements and the smell of charred wood hung in the still air. It was a long, straight street with some pubs and

7

nightclubs open; a street in which to drink and pick up a woman if you were desperate enough. Not a place to hang around aimlessly and not a street for the fainthearted. It had a reputation for desperation and enforced jollity. You just had to go there once or twice on a shore leave or you had not been to Plymouth at all. Old habits die hard.

A small group of us set out for the city centre one shining May evening not long before we were to due to sail. We were not looking for trouble, just a stroll on the Hoe and a couple of pints in Union Street on the way back. I persuaded Charlie to come with us. He was an able seaman decoder; a quiet studious man with a quick sense of humour as well as a dark side to him. He was never rude or moody, but I knew he was dreading the forthcoming voyage. I suspected that A.B. Charles Bartlett had a dread and a fear of the sea that he would reveal to nobody. He was good at his job and had the knack of getting on well with almost everyone; quite an unusual gift for a Cornishman!

As usual Charlie was bent over his diary, a bound book filled with tiny writing and diagrams.

"Come on out with us this evening Charles, 'twill do 'ee good to spend time with your mates," I demanded.

He straightened up, the spring light glinting off his large round glasses. I expected him to politely turn down my offer.

"I reckon I will, Chief, if you don't mind. I need to see a bit more of the world before I see nothing but the sea," he replied.

The day's duties being done, we changed carefully into our tiddly suits - our walking out dress. Shoes were shone and brass polished; it was a matter of pride to us to be well turned out when we went out on the town.

Walking smartly from Devonport we arrived on the Hoe with the westering sun in our eyes. As we looked out beyond Drake's island to the other side of the Tamar at Mount Edgecumbe the devastated city lay down the hill behind us. A dull roar rose from the dockyard as we tried to identify the long grey shapes of the numerous warships in the Sound.

Charlie had turned away from the sea and was looking intently inland at Kit Hill ten miles away on the horizon.

"That chimney on the hill is halfway to my home," he remarked thoughtfully.

Far out, nearly a mile from shore, lay the huge hull of a battle cruiser in the haze of the evening light. Just behind it stretched the breakwater and, on the horizon, the faint tower of the Eddystone lighthouse. Points of light winked from dancing waves but the huge ship lay inert, its guns bristling, dwarfing the other shipping dotted below us.

"Looks like the Hood to me," said Frank,

always ready with an opinion.

"Should be up near the Arctic, not sitting here in Guz," replied Charlie.

"Could be her sister ship," said Jack brightly.

"Don't be daft; she has no other ship like her. She was the only battle cruiser built to that design back in the last war. There's no other warship to touch her in any man's navy," I replied to put him in his place.

We fell silent as we stared at the long dark shape brooding out by the breakwater. There was something fantastic about the sight of our largest and most powerful ship; we could not quite believe that she was actually there before us. We knew somehow that we would never get any closer to her than we had on that sunny evening in the late spring.

We turned on our heels and wandered back down the hill to the smashed streets and ruined buildings that had been Plymouth city centre. Boarded-up shops nearly all had chalked or painted messages: "Open as usual". All the pubs in the city centre seemed to be closed or destroyed so we headed inevitably over to Union Street where the Variety Theatre loomed halfway to Devonport.

At least there was some life here on Union Street. Knots of men wandered along the wide pavement in search of pleasure. The pubs that were open stank of sweat and stale beer. The lengthening shadows reached from one side of the street to the other as we walked under the railway bridge, the occasional gaps in the buildings letting in the fading rays of the sun.

The brightness had gone out of the day. Broken glass crunched under our feet as we reached the Admiralty Arms. Once inside our eyes adjusted to the smoky gloom. We sank a couple of pints of Plymouth Brewery's best mild and bitter and prepared to move on.

A group of sailors blocked our way out. They were large men who hung together in a slightly menacing way.

"Excuse me shipmates, would you let us pass please," I asked as politely as I could.

One of the men stepped forward. He wore a filthy pea jacket covered with oil stains and torn bell bottoms. Angry red eyes glared from a pale face with a few days' growth of dark stubble.

"You can't touch us Chief. We can do what we want here and not you, not anyone, can stop us." His voice grated harshly from a throat full of gravel.

I looked at the tarnished ship's name on his stained cap.

"Stand aside please and look sharpish."

Perhaps I should not have raised my voice. A stinging slap on my cheek brought tears to my eyes. Without further thought I drove my fist into the man's stomach. The rush of air from his lungs stank of fuel oil. My eyes dropped and I saw that one of the man's shoes was missing as were three of his toes.

Once out in the street we squared up to the filthy ragged mob. There must have been eight or nine of them; each was strangely silent as he chose one of us to attack.

Charlie was the smallest and slightest of us and the first to go down, his glasses bouncing off the granite kerbstone. Miraculously they were not broken and he scooped them back as he rolled into the gutter.

The men were closing in on us. My last thought before I went down was that they should never have been allowed ashore in such a filthy condition. It's funny the thoughts you have in a crisis. Each of the men should be put on a charge for his slovenly appearance: half a leg missing here, an arm off there, blood and oil all over most of their uniforms. I grabbed a man's cap off his bald burned head and went down heavily on the gritty pavement.

By the time I stood up the group of men had gone. I did not hear them walk away; one minute they were all over us, the next they were gone.

We brushed ourselves and each other off. Miraculously no one was very much damaged. We swore and spat, straightened our caps and made our shaky way along Union Street towards Devonport and our ship.

"We should report this to the M.P.s," muttered

Frank without much conviction.

"And get ourselves put on a fizzer for brawling," replied Charlie, his glasses firmly back on his nose.

"Come on lads, let's smarten ourselves up. We won't mention this incident to a living soul if we know what's good for us," I growled. "And that's an end to it."

As we walked along our aches and pains eased rapidly. Grazed knuckles healed and bruises faded from swollen faces. By the time we were back on board ship with the long gangplank between us and Guz there was not a mark on any of us.

I walked into the wardroom to check tomorrow's duty list. The old man stood looking at me, a grave look on his face.

"Terrible news, Chief. The Hood was sunk by enemy action three days ago off Iceland, at sixty-three degrees north, thirty-eight degrees west. Of the crew of over fourteen hundred men there were only three survivors. We have lost our greatest ship and more brave men than we can afford…"

The small room swayed before me. The grey steel walls began to close in and I took a deep breath to steady myself. I resisted the urge to pull the filthy cap from my pocket and fling it down on the narrow table.

I looked the skipper straight in the eye and saluted smartly before quietly leaving the wardroom.

Back in my tiny cabin I pulled the charred cap out of my jacket and, with beating heart, looked at the filthy, oily band. I could clearly make out the tarnished letters on it depicting H.M.S. Hood.

The 9.50 to Penzance

A cold wind roared and moaned from the dark void of the November sky as the long train drove westwards across the Somerset levels. Bursts of rain cascaded down the sides of the thirteen carriages, streaking the dirty windows and hammering on the curved roofs. Dusk fell as the grey light leached out of the empty leaden landscape. From time to time the high shriek of the whistle pierced the wind-blown curtains of rain.

In the bouncing, drafty, steel cab of locomotive 6028 King George VI, Driver Seabridge and Fireman Oakes kept a keen watch for the dim green signal lights on the left hand side of the line. Oakes was relaxing a little after firing hard over the Mendip. On the right hand side of the cab Seabridge gently eased off the regulator as the train bunched slightly on a gently falling grade. Both men knew the route well and felt the pounding wheels on the rail joints register the familiar rhythm of nearly a mile-and-a-half a minute.

The dim light of an occasional isolated farm house or cottage drifted by as the heavy train crossed invisible culverts and wide rhines. The rain continued to fall in wind-blown sheets; both men strained to see the signal lights before they were obscured by the long high boiler of the powerful engine.

"Athelney, at last!" shouted Seabridge against the shattering roar of vibrating steel.

"Right you are," replied Oakes as he bent to open the wide firebox door. Soon he would be working hard firing up Wellington Bank before the long dry darkness of Whiteball Tunnel. First they would slow to negotiate Taunton; the 9.50 no longer stopped there, Exeter being the next and last stop for Seabridge and Oakes. The Penzance crew would then take over the roller coaster run of the South Devon Banks and the crossing over the Tamar into Cornwall.

The dim yellow lights of Athelney Signal Box drifted by with a cheerful wave of the green lantern from the signalman who stood on his veranda out in the wind and the rain away from his warm armchair and blazing stove. Seabridge and Oakes felt keenly the contrast between the hot firebox in front of them and the chill striking over the bucking tender behind their backs. They were used to steam engines, had cleaned and driven them all their working lives. Neither was looking forward to re-training on diesels which were about to replace the majestic Kings and Castles they drove. Each engine had a personality of its own that was well known to experienced drivers and firemen like Seabridge and Oakes.

"One thing about those diesels; nice warm cabs," shouted Oakes.

Seabridge nodded, straining to see the lights of distant Taunton in the distance. They had slowed to cross the Bristol line on the elevated girders of Cogload Junction. The canal with its line of invisible pill boxes lay to the right. Visibility was so bad and the wind so strong that neither Seabridge nor Oakes could yet make out the dark summit of the wooded Blackdown Hills to the left of Taunton.

With sheets of water blowing off the boiler King George VI slowed for the long left hand curve into Taunton. Distant lines of blurred lights twinkled in the darkness as the high shriek of the whistle pierced the gloom. Seabridge eased the train into the long platforms of Taunton Station, the yellow station lights reflected on the gleaming wet metals that stretched westwards in the darkness. The heavy locomotive jerked abruptly as it rode across the first set of points at the station throat.

Soon the long train was running alongside a wide deserted platform that stretched away to Seabridge's right. Both men craned to the right to glimpse the tiny green light of the signal high up on its pole near the platform's end.

"All clear, board's off!" shouted Oakes above the rumble of the heavy train and the gusting wind.

Although Seabridge nodded in reply his attention was diverted by a man standing close to the platform's edge. He tugged urgently on the whistle cord to warn him to stand back away from the train. For a split second he looked into the white blur of the man's face. He noticed a grease-top engineman's cap with the old familiar GWR brass badge.

Then the man stepped easily aboard the swaying engine through a blast of steam as it reached the sloped end of the platform at thirty miles an hour. He stood between Seabridge and Oakes, his stained blue overall jacket and trousers completely dry as the rain poured down on the wet track and station buildings.

Seabridge automatically pulled on the regulator to accelerate the train out of the station. He had no time to register surprise although he noticed that Oakes had seen the sudden arrival of the visitor. Both men were strangely reassured by the man's uniform overalls and wondered if he were an inspector making an unscheduled visit to their cab.

King George responded by pulling smartly away from the platform end with a sharp rhythmic bark of exhaust. The visitor stared ahead through the blurred spectacle glass, his eyes glaring with no hint of expression. Neither man spoke as the train accelerated under the Hundred Steps Bridge, shining ribbons of track fitfully gleaming to the right.

Then the man moved. Stiffly he turned and grasped the regulator with a grip of iron, his hand icy where it touched Seabridge's. He pushed it, shutting off steam from the King's massive cylinders. Despite Seabridge's frantic efforts the train began to slow.

"Fred, help me to stop this happening!" yelled the driver.

Oakes joined him on the regulator grimly struggling to keep the heavy train moving, visions of stalling on the main line in his head. Both men were sweating profusely as they heard the ominous blare of the Automatic Train Control siren go off in the cab.

"We've overshot the caution signal at on!" shouted Oakes. "I damn well missed it."

Seabridge let go of the regulator and make a rapid application of the brake even before the AWS kicked in. Ahead the red light of the down home signal shone through the murky left hand spectacle glass beside the long tapered boiler of the King. He turned in exasperation to the silent figure standing beside him as the train ground rapidly to a halt, the loco just ahead of the horizontal arm of the signal set at danger and just short of the open set of catch points.

"Good God Will, we're on the down relief line, not the down main. There'll be hell to pay now," Oakes shouted.

But Seabridge was no longer listening. A look of recognition was on his sweat stained face as he stared at the other driver's pallid features. The man turned slowly and smiled at him before a blast of air and a thunderous roar from a few feet to their right rocked the cab. The down parcels train hauled by King Henry VIII roared by with the regulator open for the long haul up Wellington Bank. A cloud of steam obscured the cab's interior as the faint red tail lamp of the parcels train receded into the rain. When the steam cleared just two shaken men were left standing in the cold cab.

The train was held safely at the signal so no further protection was necessary. Seabridge and Oakes could hear the cursing guard making his way forward along the ballast with his swaying lamp in his hand.

Finally Seabridge spoke: "What's the date, Fred?" he asked in a shaky voice.

"November 4th 1960; why do you ask?" replied Oakes.

"We're at Norton Fitzwarren, on the down relief instead of the down main. We read the wrong signal back in the station. If we had carried on we would have wrecked the train. We would be on our side in the ditch with the first half dozen coaches piled up behind our tender. The catch points would have seen to that."

"Worse still we could have swung hard onto the main line into the path of the down parcels. It doesn't bear thinking about…" replied Oakes, his voice clear against the hiss of steam and the tick of cooling metal.

"You recognised the man with us, didn't you?"

It all came out in a breathless rush: "Yes, I did. That was my Uncle Bill. I haven't seen him for twenty years. He was fireman on this very engine exactly twenty years ago when, on a night of similarly filthy weather, the wrong signal was read and the train of thirteen coaches with nine hundred people on board accelerated along the relief line instead of the main. The loco and first seven coaches were flung off the line at the catch points and thrown around like matchsticks. Uncle Bill was buried under several tons of coal from the tender and scalded to death on the left hand side of the cab…"

Ellie and Mags

What I am about to tell you defies all logic and worries me to this day, even though it only happened last year. I really should not tell you this story, because it calls into question my credibility as a teacher and as a reasonably sane human being.

My name is Alan Brown and I have taught English and History at King Edward VI Community College in Totnes for a number of years. I am form tutor to 7 Churchward 2, and particularly enjoy the pastoral part of my job, helping young people to grow up and to acquire the study skills necessary to see them through GCSEs and beyond.

The new Year 7 curriculum is an exciting one, integrating humanity and science subjects to develop lively minds, at least in theory! I had a hand in writing the History and English project based on Berry Pomeroy Castle. As a result I presided over the forthcoming visit to the castle and the preparatory lessons preceding it.

We studied the history of the castle: why it was

built, when it was built and what happened when the Norman de Pomerais handed it over to the Seymours. We studied the transition from fortress to mansion, from defensive to domestic architecture. We shuddered at the eerie legends that persist to this day concerning both the Seymour and de Pomerai families.

At last the day came for the visit to Berry Pomeroy Castle. My form and I gathered in the form room with drinks and sandwiches, waterproof anoraks, clipboards with pen, pencil and paper and money for ice creams at the Castle café, all the things important to twelve-year-old students. I had first aid kit, epi pens, mobile phone, medical details of students with special needs, and all necessary permission slips. While I waited for the two Teaching Assistants and Mrs Albertson to come across the road I took the register.

"Put that drink away please Tamsin. Quiet please everyone. Answer your names clearly please. Don't say anything if you're not here.

Sally Atkins…
Jordon Pearce…
Simon Pengelly…
Ellie Pomeroy…
Mags Pomeroy…"

While we waited for a few students to go to the loo I considered the Pomeroy twins. They were old fashioned in the best sense, devoted to each other in a way that only twins could be. They lived on a farm near the village of Berry Pomeroy and must have known all about the castle. They were always attentive and well behaved, asking intelligent questions about the history and legends with no sense of condescension or superiority. They were good sports, who looked after each other and always watched out for each other, as if it were their second nature to do so. They were very pretty in an innocent way, and altogether good and conscientious students.

We made the short journey to the castle in the two battered school minibuses. Soon we made the sharp turn from the narrow lane, past the three cottages, and down the winding wooded hill to the clearing where the castle stood on its crag surrounded by ancient beech and newer larch trees. We were suddenly in a remote world with Totnes miles away and the past a tangible entity.

The students were strangely quiet as they got out of the minibuses and looked at the tall trees with a gentle breeze touching their tops. We sat on the wide sun-dappled lawn facing the curtain walls with their ramparts, the twin towers of the gatehouse and the high ruins of the Tudor mansion which seemed to frown from behind the walls.

"Listen up, everyone. Make sure that you remain in your group of four, and be aware that there are steep drops into the valley on the far side of the castle. You are here to do three things in any order you like. Draw a rough diagram of the castle, pacing out distances, and label it; draw a careful sketch of any part of the castle that appeals most to you, and write a short story based on any aspect of the history of the castle that you like. Do not climb on the walls or raise your voices at any time. Do not run or drop any litter. The loos are behind the café. Ask any of us if you have any questions. Remember that there is no such thing as a silly question if you really want to know the answer.

"And if you see the ghost of Lady Margaret, ask her if you may help her," I added to Annie the Teaching Assistant, a remark I later had cause to regret.

I presented the educational group pass to the English Heritage curator and we entered the castle together, an orderly group slightly overawed by our surroundings. I think that it was the remoteness that has this effect on us. That and the contrast to the former bustle of the busy classroom a handful of miles away.

The inner courtyard of the castle was a bumpy grass area surrounded by high walls on two sides, the ruined mansion on the third and ragged pillars of stone on the side overlooking the steep valley. According to legend, the Roundhead bombardment had all but destroyed the castle walls and the mansion range that

26

led from the kitchens to the great hall in the main block.

We split into groups; some to explore the ramparts and chapel in the gatehouse, some to look at the massive kitchen block with its huge fireplaces now open to the sky, and some to wander around the rooms and courtyard of the roofless mansion ruin, whose granite window frames rose high overhead.

Excited voices could be heard arguing about this and that, but all the students were hard at work completing their assignments. Soon it was time for Annie and I to go to the café outside the castle. We sat in the sun facing the twin towers of the gatehouse, the high ramparts and the remote round tower at their right hand end.

"That's funny," said Annie. "I could swear that there is glass in the windows of the round tower. There certainly wasn't a moment ago."

I looked at the roofless tower beyond the lawn where the moat used to be. Sure enough, I could make out the shimmer of diamond panes contained within the granite window frames.

Then I heard the first voice raised in anger floating shrilly across the lawn.

"I know you fancy him Mags! You can't deny it, you little bitch! But I love Tom much more than you ever will…"

A loud shriek sent us both running towards the

27

gatehouse and along the rampart walk to the tower. There stood the lone figure of Ellie in great distress, tears running down her pale face. She was sobbing so hard that she could hardly speak, and shaking uncontrollably. Finally she turned to me and sank down onto the stone floor of the round tower room. Mutely she pointed to the head of the spiral stone staircase that turned out of sight to the darkness below.

"I don't know what came over me. I... I pushed her. Down there. I heard her fall. I don't know what we're going to do..."

Her eyes rolled up into her head as she passed out on the cool floor of the tower room. I looked at Annie with a growing realisation of what had happened.

"Phone for an ambulance as soon as you can, and look after Ellie. I must go down there," I said in a shocked voice.

With a heavy heart I set off down the slippery stone steps into the dungeon-like ground floor room of the tower. I expected at every turn to see a sprawling smashed body with limbs twisted at crazy angles and blood everywhere.

I was almost more shocked to find an empty round room with a small fireplace and a smell of damp earth. Of Mags Pomeroy there was no sign, no trace at all.

I knew that Ellie had pushed her, but where on

earth was her beloved sister? I searched all over the castle and organised groups to look for her. I alerted the custodian who looked in all the hiding places known to her. Finally I phoned the police and notified the school. We were utterly mystified; there was no place for 'vanished off the face of the earth', despite *Picnic at Hanging Rock*, on the risk assessment form we had so carefully filled in as part of our thorough preparations for the visit.

Ellie had regained consciousness and was taken away in an ambulance. She had not said a word and seemed to be in deep shock, eyes staring from the palest of faces. Groups of her friends stood tearfully together as the ambulance drove carefully away. A stunned silence prevailed. No one wanted to look directly at anyone else.

No sign of Mags was ever found. The search for her grew: the ponds near the castle were dragged, lines of searchers walked slowly through the woods and over the hills, all road and rail links in and out of Devon were examined. Reports of sightings came from as far away as Perth and Penzance but no trace of the little girl was ever found. The nation-wide search spread abroad, but foundered in a fog of supposition.

The Pomeroy family were left to grieve in private. I was offered counselling but turned it down on the grounds that I certainly could have done nothing in my power to prevent the tragic disappearance of

Mags. Ellie eventually recovered, but would never talk about what had happened. Her mind had mercifully blanked out the mysterious events of the day her twin sister vanished.

That is not the end of the story, however. A few months after our summer visit to the castle something very strange happened. Tom, the Pomeroy's cowman, who had only recently left school in Totnes, was badly injured when his motorbike swerved suddenly into a tree in the lane close to the entrance to Berry Pomeroy Castle.

During the long recovery process in Torbay Hospital he was interviewed several times by the police. His story never changed; there were no traces of drugs or alcohol in what had been left of his blood before massive transfusions set him on the path to eventual recovery.

He was a good lad, a careful worker and a very good employee. He said that as he was driving home after work, past the castle entrance, a young girl stepped out of the hedge directly in front of his bike. He had no time to stop, and passed right through her. There was no impact and he clearly remembered the girl's face before he hit her and swerved into the tree.

"It was Mags. Of that I am absolutely certain, cross my heart. But she was no living girl. Her face held no expression. It could not have been Ellie because, after her recovery, she had been taken out of school in Totnes and sent to a girls' boarding school in Newton Abbot. And no, I was not aware that either girl had a crush on me. Had I been so I would certainly not have encouraged it. I am totally mystified by the whole business…"

I Shall Be With You

He came to me again last night in a dream as I slept soundly in my chamber. He was a mass priest, a small, youngish man with something of the sixteenth century about him. He spoke to me in a faint voice, the unmistakable accent of Barnstaple coming to me across the centuries. But he was no ghost; his eyes searched me out, seeming to bore into my undecided soul.

I was not the least afraid of this priest. I felt that he was earnestly trying to help me. He did not say his name or where he had come from. All he said was: "Hold fast to the old faith in the Blessed Trinity. I shall be there at the hour of your death…"

I was not a particularly religious man. Like my priestly visitor my name was not important. My main concern at the moment was my younger brother Anthony: suave, rakish Anthony. If any man needed the attention of a priest it was he.

Anthony had always been the black sheep of the family. He was handsome, charming and talented, but profligate and easily led. It is as if he could not help himself. His life had always been a confused pickle of missed appointments, lost opportunities, lost weekends, fast women and loose cars. Like me he was a writer, but with a far superior talent. The only major thing we really had in common was an abiding love of the poetry of Charles Causley. We were both members of the Causley Society in the hilltop town of Launceston.

Last week we drove independently to an evening of poetry at the Eagle House Hotel in Launceston. Anthony and I lived in different parts of Plymouth. I phoned him to offer him a lift but he declined, saying that he had some unfinished business at home after the poetry evening. I wondered what the unfortunate husband of the lady he was seeing would have to say about that.

So we left Plymouth independently, he in his nasty bulbous Audi TT and me in my dented relic of the '90s. It was a beautiful evening as I drove towards Launceston on the A388. Blackbirds sang in the trees and a froth of cow parsley covered the verges. Fluffy clouds floated above the chimney on Kit Hill as the smell of pasties announced Callington. The rampart of Bodmin Moor rose to my left as the road became narrower, more winding and more interesting.

The sun was still high in the sky as I reached the outskirts of Launceston. I carefully dropped down through the narrow streets, through the Southgate arch, and round to the Georgian glory of the Eagle House Hotel, perched between the imposing mound of the castle and the valley below. I saw my brother's car parked in front of the hotel and drove slowly up the hill towards the castle gatehouse. Beside the gatehouse was a small stable yard where I parked the car hard by the walls.

There was half an hour before the poetry evening and I walked through the gatehouse arch to admire the view of the countryside from the castle green. I read the historical plaque on the damp gatehouse wall that explained the former grim function of the building. It had been a prison, a dungeon called 'Doomsdale', which had held within its grey walls such notables as George Fox and St Cuthbert Mayne.

It was a relief to emerge onto green lawns and meet my brother silhouetted against the wide north Cornish sky. He turned to me, a troubled look on his handsome face.

"Thomas," he said without any preamble. "I've really led a very dissolute life. Things have got to change. Nearly every night I dream of a priest who beseeches me to turn to God. This evening I have a late appointment with Father O'Malley in Plymouth. I will be received into the Catholic Church and begin a new life repenting of my sins. And not before time…"

I was staggered, quite devoid of breath for a moment.

"Well Anthony, thanks for telling me. I must say that I'm tremendously relieved and happy for you. What more can I say?"

At that moment I can honestly say that I had never felt closer to my wicked brother. The straight and narrow would be a struggle for him but I was sure that he would be all right sooner rather than later.

We took a turn around the town before the poetry evening. Together we walked through the opposite castle gatehouse and up the hill to the town square. The quarterjacks in the town hall struck the quarter and I found myself humming an old hymn tune.

> "By the light of burning martyrs
> Christ thy bleeding feet we track…"

A lovely mixed metaphor, I thought.

As we stood at the far end of the square facing the White Hart I could feel the roar of an invisible crowd all round me. My misted vision cleared and I saw a tall gallows on the cobbles in front of me. Many of the buildings were the same but shabbier and more decrepit. The crowd grew silent and pressed in on every side as a slightly built man, the priest who had repeatedly come to me in my dreams, was drawn under the gallows on a cart. A rope was placed around his neck, prayers were said by a bearded chaplain and a loud question was addressed to the lonely bound figure high on the cart. The little priest shook his head and the cart was whipped forward leaving him dangling in the air. Feeling faint I pitched forward into the stink of the crowd. A space was cleared around me and as my vision swam back into focus I saw some words carved into the pavement in front of me.

"Hey, steady on!" cried Anthony, bending down to help me up.

"On this spot on November 29th 1577, Blessed Cuthbert Mayne was Hanged, Drawn and Quartered for his Catholic Faith," he read aloud. "That figures."

We hurried down the hill to the Eagle House, slipped into the hall just in time. The evening went wonderfully well; we were absorbed by the complex poetry of a very straightforward man and left in the warm dusk for the drive back to Plymouth.

Anthony paused before getting into his car.

"Are you sure you're all right, Tom?" he asked me in a concerned voice.

"Of course I am, Anthony. I had a funny turn back in the square, that's all. I haven't been sleeping too well recently. Drive carefully, won't you. You go on ahead, I'll be right behind you."

Anthony said something to me that he had never said before: "Bless you, Thomas."

I walked back up the hill to the castle gatehouse looming in the dusk. As I unlocked the door of my car I realised that I had parked where the actual prison had once stood. I shuddered momentarily at the cruelty of Queen Elizabeth's reign. Such mind dominance back then must have amounted to terrorism today. I slid into my car which was filled with the sharp tang of incense.

A bad case of writer's imagination, I thought as I started the car and switched on the lights which played on the grim damp walls of Doomsdale.

There isn't much more to tell. The story should have ended there, but unfortunately it didn't. It would have been a very happy ending: Anthony's change of heart and new life leading to many years of brotherly companionship.

I followed Anthony out of the town. He was driving more slowly than usual and had picked up a passenger. I assumed it was someone Anthony knew from the evening and had offered him a lift back to Plymouth. Anyway, he was engaged in a lively conversation with his passenger who was sitting in the front seat huddled in some sort of cloak, or so it appeared. Something about the angle of his head was familiar, although at the time I couldn't quite put my finger on it.

Before Treburley there was a series of sharp bends on a mainly wooded stretch of the road.

Anthony was driving with uncharacteristic care in front of me, his headlights swinging ahead round the bends.

Suddenly I caught a glimpse of a pair of yellow eyes on the road in front of Anthony's car. He swerved instinctively to miss the animal in front of him and smashed through the wooden barrier, plunging off the road into the woods. In a panic I stopped the car and flung open the door to hear a succession of crashes as the car smashed down through the trees. There was a moment of silence and then a tremendous explosion as the car hit a huge tree. The orange fireball rose rapidly above the canopy of leaves and branches, the searing heat struck my face. All I could do was call the emergency services in a halting voice on my mobile phone.

When the wreck had cooled, what was left of my brother was removed from the car. His identity was checked from dental records and he was buried in the family plot in Weston Mill Cemetery. His funeral service was taken by Father O'Malley who also buried the passenger whose charred body could be identified by no dental records.

The only distinguishing features left on the corpse were the burned remains of a rope around the neck and a crucifix twisted by heat clutched in the claw of the right hand.

Limehouse Lane

That afternoon was beastly hot; as I walked down the lane to the river the brassy heat lay like a shroud on the land. The hedges were thick with dust, even the nettles and brambles were coated. My sandals raised little eddies of fine powder as I walked. The choking dust was in my scalp, on my skin and in my eyes.

I could see the tracks of my family in the dust. They had gone ahead to the relative coolness of the creek where overhanging trees provided some shade from the merciless sun. I would catch them up at the lane's end.

The stifling heat seemed trapped by the lane's high hedges. The occasional tree provided momentary shade. I walked slowly on, conserving what little energy I had in my core. I rounded a corner of the sloping hollow path. Flies buzzed around my head and I heard a deeper drone as I saw a dense cloud ahead of me.

Then I saw it, not quite believing it was there. A humped shape lay in the dust across the narrow lane.

As I approached the thick cloud of flies rose heavily and dissipated. I broke into a shambling trot. Could my wife have fainted in the heat? If so then surely one of the boys would have come back to fetch me.

What lay in the dust was easily the most unpleasant thing that I had ever seen. Sprawled on the ground was what appeared to be a mummy, a ghastly dried husk of a man. Any fluids contained within the cadaver had long drained into the dust leaving a skeletal form from which rags of clothing hung in tatters. The eyes had long gone; the mouth had dried open in a dusty scream. Bony limbs seemed flung out from the protruding rib cage. The hands clawed upwards while the feet were carelessly crossed. One of the feet had become detached from the bony knob of an ankle.

I stood near the corpse paralysed by the cold chill of horror. The flies and bees had stopped buzzing and the lane had fallen utterly silent. The thing was blocking my way to the river. It couldn't have been there when my wife and family walked down to the river a few minutes earlier. It lay on the imprint of their shoes in the dust. Beyond it the tracks lay evenly spaced.

How could I get past it? It sprawled untidily across the track blocking my way; I could not step over it or go round it. I imagined it gathering itself in the dust to sit up and croak at me, or cunningly grab my ankle as I tried to go round it. All things had become possible except getting to the other side of it. I couldn't climb up into the hedge with my sandals and shorts on; the brambles and nettles would soon inflict a flaming agony on my bare legs. I could not go back and cut through the fields, too many thistles and nettles would make short work of me.

I forced myself to look once again at the body. Of course! It had dropped from the ash tree above. A frayed length of sisal binder cord was knotted around the shrivelled throat.

I had to get on! My wife would wonder where I was and set off back up the lane to look for me. The thing was real, a nasty dried-up corpse not an apparition. She must not see it – I must make sure of that. I was beginning to get angry; a bundle of bones was not going to get the better of me!

I took a step forward and swung my foot at the thing blocking my way. I expected to hear a dry crunch like the rattle of old sticks as the corpse was booted to the side of the lane. Instead I felt an icy chill shoot up my leg and I shut my eyes tightly. When I opened them again the thing was gone. There was no indication of the shape that had lain in the dust at my feet, no outline of a barely human shape on the lane's dusty surface.

I stepped carefully over the vacant spot and walked on a few paces. There, thirty yards in front of me, was a figure coming up the lane towards me, its outline wavering in the heat. It didn't look quite human. I did however recognise the voice calling a distant, "Hello."

The figure came nearer and I saw from the knobbly stick and green Plymouth Argyle shirt that it was Dave Dunsford, a retired farmer who lived near me up in the village.

He looked carefully at me.

"You've seen it too, haven't you? I can tell. I don't want to talk about it here because it might come back. You come round to my house when you're all back in the village and I'll tell you what I know. Come on your own though."

"Thank you, Dave," I managed to say. "I'll see you later then."

Still feeling a clammy chill I walked down the searing lane with puffs of dust rising lazily round my feet. The flies had returned and I could hear the wood pigeons in a distant copse. Soon I heard splashing and voices from the creek below me and knew that everything was all right.

After a rest under the overhanging trees and a few games of ducks and drakes, skimming flat stones over the placid surface of the water, the sluggish tide began to turn and we made our weary way back up the dusty lane in the heat.

After tea in the relative cool of the evening I

walked up the slope to Dave's tidy bungalow on the edge of the village. He let me in and sat me down in the front room with its view of the church behind the gardens. It was hard to believe that we had both seen something so foul a few hours earlier.

Dave looked gravely at me, his face more drawn than usual.

"Back in the long, hot summer of '59 young Rufus Putt from number ten Holly Villas fell madly in love with Rosie Dunsford, a cousin of mine from over behind Harberton. It was hopeless really. Rosie had set her mind to go up country and soon enough she did, running off with that Sam Skedgell from Bowden. It didn't do her no good though; she's back in Follaton now surrounded by grandchildren who get into no end of scrapes.

"When the same young Rufus left his job on Ralph's farm and disappeared, no-one went looking for him because they thought that he had followed Rosie up country. In truth he had got himself a bit of binder twine and gone down Limehouse Lane to top himself.

"What he did was to climb the big ash tree, tie one end of the binder cord round a high branch, the other end round his neck and jump. He hung up in the crown of that tree all through the hot summer until the autumn wind stripped off the leaves. When the cord rotted through down he came in a heap into the lane. It was Farmer Soper who found him and he was never quite the same again. His wife died suddenly a few weeks after.

"Rufus comes back for a reason. I see him because I am related to Rosie. Why you saw him I just don't know. Perhaps it was some kind of warning."

After a brief talk I thanked Dave and left the bungalow still mystified. I walked home in the cooling dusk past number ten Holly Villas and sat down to talk to my wife. I told her that I had seen a ghost, but told her none of the details except for the fact that Rufus had been jilted.

My wife looked troubled. Her eyes clouded.

"There is something I have been meaning to tell you. It's all over now but last summer I met..."

Major Wiley

When Major Wiley finally died most of the village heaved a heartfelt sigh of relief. He had lived for years at the Hermitage, cared for in his long infirmity by a wizened monkey of a man who had been Wiley's batman during the war. Nobody had the faintest idea how old Wiley had been when he died; nobody had actually been close to him in all the years he lived in the village.

He was a remote man with nothing likeable about him. He sneered and scowled when he came into contact with the villagers and never had a good word to say about anything. He was tall and high-shouldered with a prickly ginger moustache on his long upper lip. His gaze was icy and distant and he only smiled if he had thoroughly upset someone. When he spoke, and he rarely did, his voice was curiously high-pitched with a faint Midland intonation. Reclusive to the last, he died suddenly the night of the thunderstorm.

The villagers were most surprised when it was announced in church that Major Wiley's funeral would be at three o'clock in the afternoon of the following Friday. While alive he had never entered the church and it was well known that he was an atheist.

"I expect the old bastard wanted to upset as many of us as he could by being carried up the village and into the church in a box," remarked Mrs Putt. "I've heard that no-one from the undertakers is involved and that his servant is preparing his body for burial."

When the afternoon of the funeral arrived quite a crowd had gathered near the church steps out of curiosity. A few were there to pray for his soul; most wanted to make sure that he was actually dead.

The single bell was tolled high in the tower. An icy east wind sprang up as four old men dressed in rusty black, whom nobody had seen before, appeared at the gate of the Hermitage carrying the mortal remains of Major Wiley in a black coffin. They set off bearing their burden up the hill past the war memorial to the church steps.

"A black coffin, how appropriate," said Mrs Treddaway in an unusually acid tone.

The bearers appeared to be struggling as they came up the hill. Old Trelawney, the Major's former batman, led them, his long arms swinging at his side. The consensus of the waiting crowd was that 'things were not quite right'.

The cortege paused briefly to catch their breath at the foot of the steps that led up to the lychgate.

Trelawney appeared to mutter something out of the side of his mouth and the men began to mount the steps with the heavy coffin slanted on their shoulders. They had almost reached the top, where they would slide the coffin onto the slate slab and take a breather, when one of the bearers slipped off a step.

The inevitable gasp came from the tense group of villagers. In slow motion the black coffin started to slide off the men's shoulders. For a split second it was airborne before landing on the steps with a rending crash. Two or three women shrieked as the lid splintered and slid off sideways.

As the coffin slid to rest at an angle at the foot of the steps the lid clattered down beside it. Those who had the nerve to look into the dark void did not see what they had expected to see. Lying in the casket was no still figure with arms crossed over the chest and lips and eyelids sewn shut but two hessian bags of stones.

Another gasp emanated from the crowd and all eyes were lifted to the bearers at the top of the steps. They had gone, melted away into empty air. All that was left was Trelawney sitting on the slab with his head in his hands. The crowd melted silently away to leave him there with his despair. He had never sought help before and none was forthcoming at this hour. Soon the siren of a police car coming down the hill at speed into the village burst onto the silent scene.

Detective Sergeant Jim Carter of Devon and

Cornwall CID glanced warily at the small man hunched apelike on the chair across the scarred desk in front of him in the interview room. He saw a man who was incredibly old, but not unpleasant in character.

"I have to warn you that concealing a body after death is a very serious offence," said Carter.

"It would be so much simpler if I had hidden it," replied Trelawney. "Then I would take the punishment and eventually it would all be over and done with. The truth is not so simple; it will take a long time to explain and then you probably won't believe me..."

Carter thought that the solution would be simpler than that. He had already obtained a search warrant and a team of skilled police officers were hard at work searching the Hermitage and its tangled garden at that very moment. Two hours later he had to concede that Trelawney had a valid point and was even beginning to doubt his own sanity.

This is roughly what Trelawney told him as the rising wind roared through the tops of the high trees outside the police station:

"It all began a long time ago, Sir. Major Wiley was adopted soon after he was born in Leamington. His parents were called Crowley and his older brother was Aleister, better known as the Great Beast 666, an adept of the Black Arts and a very bad man indeed. Young Frank began to exhibit the same traits from a

50

very early age and his parents, in despair, put him up for adoption. They were not bad people, very religious, and just couldn't handle two potential Satanists in the family.

Frank was brought up by the Wiley family and took their name. He went to Cambridge where he was sent down from Caius College for a number of very serious offences. At the beginning of the war he was commissioned into the Black Watch. He found the Army to his liking, being utterly ruthless and hating the Germans as he did.

In 1940, when home on leave, he met up with his brother Aleister who was old and infirm by then. They formed a pact in Eastbourne in Aleister's rooms. Frank undertook to carry on where his older brother had left off. He would perform rites and sacrifices which would make him invincible. His strong will would determine the course of the rest of his life. In return for total power over his fellow men and a very long life on earth satisfying his every desire and whim he effectively sold his soul to Satan, his lord and master. He had become invincible and practically immortal.

His sinister pact was put to the test in Normandy in June 1944. Just inland from Sword Beach he was struck directly by a shell. I saw it with my own eyes. One minute he was standing looking through his field glasses, the next he was blown to pieces. If you don't believe me look at this."

Trelawney reached into the evidence tray and pulled out a greasy leather wallet. He handed three small photographs to Carter who looked with horror at the first.

What he saw was the top half of an officer who was unmistakably Wiley. The face was clearly identifiable as were the three pips of a captain on the shoulders. Here all resemblance to humanity ended. The outflung arms were as untouched as the head; the body below the open chest cavity had ceased to exist. A mass of tangled entrails completed the picture. *Thank heavens colour photography was still in its infancy*, thought a shocked Carter.

He looked at the other two photographs. An intact Wiley now wore a major's crown on his shoulder and a slightly older Wiley, still in battledress, had been promoted to Lieutenant Colonel. The man could not have survived the shell, so what on earth was going on?

Trelawney was sent home on bail and told to remain in the area. No sign of Wiley was found either at the Hermitage or its vicinity. Eventually Trelawney was summoned back to the police station.

"Now Sir, the time has come for some plain speaking. What did you do with the body of Major Frank Wiley on the night of his death?" asked a stern Carter.

"I will swear to what I am about to tell you in the highest court in the land, but I don't expect you to believe it. I'm not even sure if *I* do." The little man's brown eyes bored into Carter's.

"The night of the thunderstorm Frank was breathing with great difficulty. I knew that, despite the pact, he was not long for this world. Satan had had enough of him and, liar that he is, had decided to do away with him.

"At last it was over. I knew it when the time came. Frank's eyes turned a fiery red and he just stopped breathing. I went to close his eyes and he began to fade. As I watched he gradually faded away until only a depression was to be seen in the bed and he was gone.

"Something had to be done. I arranged the funeral at the church so that everyone would believe that things were normal. But I don't know who the four bearers were who carried him up to the church. They just turned up at the house and proceeded to take the coffin away. When it came time to enter holy ground they could not manage it and they dropped the coffin. I was the one who put the bags of stones inside. I had to in order to make up the weight.

"After the funeral I was going to vanish as well, before death certificates and probate were demanded. Now it's too late and I swear that I've told you the whole truth."

Carter was dumbfounded. There was nothing that this man could be charged with; he would have to let him go. As the little man walked out of the interview room Carter found himself offering up a prayer for the black soul of Major Wiley.

Return of the Native

A man on his way into the churchyard with a spade and a wooden stake in his hand always raises a certain amount of suspicion in the casual observer. George, however, was no casual observer but a churchwarden. He greeted me with enthusiasm.

"It's good of you to do this," he said. "We need the space for the cremations and those old stones are very much in the way."

"I'll take great care and set the stones I find upright," I replied as I opened the churchyard gate and walked up the path to the oak tree at the far corner.

The flat stones marking the recent cremations lay in rows under the shade of the oak. They were diminutive compared to the older grave markers in their rows and the occasional table tomb. The oak tree spread its branches over the area of the churchyard between the tower and a steep drop into the gardens. The cremation stones lay on a plateau, a shelf between the church and the village below.

A few weeks earlier Mr Edmonds the undertaker had struck stone while digging a slot for the latest cremation. He had carefully peeled back the turf to reveal the date 1860 and some letters incised in a large piece of slate that lay almost a foot underground. Not wishing to disturb what was there he had replaced the turf and watered it back in. Mr Pengelly's ashes had been planted at the end of a new row and the problem of what to do with the subterranean slate passed on to the churchwardens. Because I was a few years younger than George I volunteered for the job of bringing to light the long buried slab and setting it upright again.

I poked in the dry soil with the wooden stake until I found the edge of the slate a few inches below the turf. Then I cut the turf in a straight line a few inches to the side of the underground slab. Carefully peeling back the turf I gradually uncovered the dark slate. With the flat of the spade I curled the dry turf back until I had uncovered the whole of the slate that lay at a slight slant into the soil.

It was still impossible to read the inscription because of the dark stain of the dry earth. I brushed the soil off and wiped the slate clean. Gradually the inscription emerged as the soil crumbled away. It read as follows:

Sacred to the memory of
RICHARD CRIPER
who departed this life on
2nd November 1859
and his wife
ANNE CRIPER
Who unwillingly followed on
2nd November 1860.

**Forgive them Lord,
for they know not what they do.**

"Most curious," remarked George from close behind me. I jumped at the intrusion. "Quite a stern judgement on that stone. I wouldn't be surprised if people think that we should have left it buried."

"It's done now," I said. "The secret's out, whatever it means. I have no idea what was intended by the cryptic inscription, but I would like to find out."

"You might not like what you find, be prepared for that. Let me know what you come up with," said George before turning and walking back towards the lychgate.

I sat back on my haunches. Something was making me increasingly reluctant to lever the stone out of its shallow hole and set it upright. I let it lie like a partly-exhumed corpse while I considered what to do next.

Tomorrow I would pull it out and set it into a deep slot that I would dig to set it upright. I would gently scrub the earth off and wipe the inscription with a greasy clump of old sheep's wool to erase the scratches. Then I would go to the museum and look up the records of the Criper family.

As I stood laboriously up the sun emerged from a rack of clouds to the west. The rays slanted in a sickly way catching the side of the tree but leaving the stone in deep shadow. I turned away from my work and walked back down the path to the lychgate.

The orange light of the setting sun cast my shadow onto the rough stone wall of the church. It must have been a trick of the somewhat eldritch light that there appeared to be two shadows gliding along the red sandstone of the wall, flickering over the buttresses as I walked and casting their identical elongations up the dusty diamonds of the leaded windows.

I slept well that night although my wife called out once or twice in the night in her sleep. I made out the name 'Richard' more than once. In the morning she was unable to tell me what her dreams had been about.

Next day I set the heavy stone upright and cleaned it, unable to shake off the feeling that I was being watched. *A silly reaction to reading too much M R James*, I thought. I found a few small pieces of bone in the soil that I excavated for the stone: bits of flaky rib and yellowish knuckle bones which I put back in the hole with the stone. Then I set off for Totnes on my bike.

Fortunately the study room at the back of the Elizabethan House was open. I settled down in a crumbling armchair with a monograph entitled: *Some Observations on the Remarkable Events Surrounding the Deaths of Mr and Mrs Richard Criper of the Parish of Ashprington in the Year of Our Lord 1860 by the Revd. Percival Warleggan MA (Cantab.), Rector of the Above Parish.*

The piece was well written and reasonably short. It was written by an educated man who managed to share his sense of wonder at the strange events that he observed in his parish one hundred and fifty years ago.

It transpired the Richard Criper, the estate steward, was a jealous and manipulative man who was stricken with consumption in early middle age. On his deathbed he confided to the Rector that he would come back from the dead to take his wife, Anne, back with him to the eternal realms. Revd. Warleggan was horrified and tried to persuade the man to recant his heretical and selfish intentions. He failed to do so and Criper died a difficult death on All Souls' Day with his intentions locked firmly in his terminally-wheezing chest.

His widow Anne became a haunted shell of her former self. From time to time she confided in the Rector that Richard had returned for her, but that she had resisted – had been too strong for the spectre to influence her. In fact she had resisted with anger. But as the year went on she appeared diminished and increasingly frail, her dark and determined eyes burning in a wasted and prematurely aged face.

Then the inevitable happened, just as the Rector knew it would despite all his prayers and candles, on the day of year's mind of Richard's death. He was called to Anne Criper's bedside by the neighbour Mrs Putt.

"I fear that Mistress Criper's a-breathing of her last. 'Er's whisht and bad and will soon, I fear, be as dead as a rag. Us must go to 'en and smooth her path to 'Eaven, Reverend Sir."

The shrunken figure in the bed glared up at Warleggan as he said the last Rites and anointed the Holy Oils.

"'Ee's come for I at last, the old bastard, just as us knawed 'ee would. Promise me one thing, though. Mark my name and date on the stone and then lay 'n flat on the ground so that the grass may grow over 'n and the name of Criper be laid to rest and well forgotten. Do this so that us can rest in the light of the Lord away from the influence of the Dark man."

At this she exhausted herself and breathed her last; her shrunken body became smaller and lighter and dwarfed by the tumbled sheets of her deathbed.

Quite a story, I thought. I did not doubt the Reverend's faith or sincerity but felt that his judgement must have been clouded by the superstition of the day and the close contact with uneducated country people, despite his Cambridge theological training. Had I but realised it at the time I could not have been more wrong.

When I returned home I had the feeling that there was someone waiting for me in the cottage. Indeed muddy footprints led up the path into the unusually open front door. Not pausing to remember that it had not rained for the past month-and-a-half I burst in on the intruder in my own house.

A slim, wasted man sat in my armchair behind the door. He did not rise when I came angrily in on him. He was slight with long pale hands and rough clothes of an antique cut. Most of all I resented his hobnailed boots that had smeared mud on my worn carpet. But I was drawn to his thin, lined face from which blazed light blue eyes of an unearthly intensity.

His voice reached me from a long way away.

"Now, good Zur, you have taken the liberty of bringing to light our stone and our sad history which was better left buried. We may not rest until this wrong be righted. You will tell it to the world and our secret will be abroad for all to comment on. We cannot allow for this to happen…"

I blinked in shock and the outline of the figure wavered. My heart seemed to drop like a stone as I summoned up the desperate courage to address the man in my chair.

"You don't have the power to frighten me, Mr Criper. You're not real, you can no longer influence anything."

The wan features creased into a smile that was certainly not pleasant.

"You could be right there, Zur. But I may no longer have to do so. The fact is that you died of a heart attack about three minutes past and now you, Anne and I will keep company for eternity…"

Silly Cat

I am a prolific dreamer who has serial dreams about places I have never visited in my waking life. Often my dreams make perfect sense; when they don't I can often wake myself up in order to end them. A few weeks after my mother's funeral I dreamed this dream.

One spring evening I was standing in the centre of the village outside the Newtons' house looking into a skip. I looked up to see a familiar figure walking down the hill past the war memorial in the evening light. My mother was coming down to talk to me; this would have been perfectly normal if she had still been alive...

I always got on particularly well with my mother. She was tall and strong and very practical. From time to time during my young life I would dream about her and the events in the dream often came true. When she entered her middle eighties her health began to decline and she became progressively deaf. When she died at the age of eighty-eight it was a relief to her;

a lifetime of hard work on the land and in gardens had taken its toll. She had been ready to go and was most disappointed that she was still alive the last time she came home from the hospital.

When her father died back in 1956 she felt terrible because we had recently moved down to Devon from Bucks and she had not had the chance to see him before he went. He came back to reassure her that he was fine and told her not to worry or fret. She heard his voice in the middle of the night in the kitchen of the flat in Tuckenhay. Consequently she knew that he was at rest and was able to carry on with her life.

Here she was in the light of a spring evening walking down the hill to see me. I noticed that she was much more upright and that she now walked practically without a limp. She carried her stick but no longer relied on it except to keep the odd stray dog away with her characteristic, "Goo lie down!"

As she drew nearer I saw that she looked quite well although rather tired.

"Hello," I said. "I haven't seen you for a while. You look well. What's it like in Heaven?"

"It's all right," she replied. "But I must say that it took a bit of getting used to."

We talked in a relaxed way, as if talking to one's dead mother were quite the most natural thing in the world. Then my mother looked directly at me.

"Your cat Hoskins is going to have a bit of a

problem. She will be most peculiar for a while but will come out of it on top. We won't know if she has been hit by a car or shaken by a dog but the only physical effect will be a bruise on the buttock."

I leaned on the corner of the skip. My mother was very good with cats although she never got on particularly well with Mrs Hoskins our black and white farm cat. She also had an expression she used when talking about an especially tiresome English female of a type that she did not appreciate. "Silly cat!" she'd say and that was that. Being half American, and having been brought up in France, my mother always found certain types of English people a little hard to take.

And so the conversation ended. My mother said goodbye, assured me that she was fine and said that it would be a while before we met again. So I went home and told my family about the conversation.

After that dream life went on with work and play, church and gardening and all the good things of village life. Then it happened; we couldn't find Hoskins anywhere. The three of us looked down the garden, in the woodshed and in the cellar. No sign of our black and white Hoskins.

Two days dragged by and I found myself thinking that the loss of Hoskins was almost as hard to bear as the loss of my mother. We had had the cat for twelve years and thought we knew all her ways. But a cat can always surprise you.

We began to catch a glimpse of her outside the house and in the neighbours' gardens. She would not let us get near her, only staring at us with wide frantic eyes and ears flat to her skull. She began to get weak and Tom found her hidden behind some junk in the cellar. He was able to pick her up and bring the poor bedraggled animal into the house where she sat tensely on my lap and would hardly eat at all. She was clearly badly traumatised and so we bundled her into the cat basket and took her off to the vet. We had noticed her dragging one of her hind legs and so wanted her examined.

The vet held Hoskins on the examining table and felt her all over. The cat relaxed somewhat, no longer appearing to care what fate had in store for her. Kidney function was fine, she was a bit thin. As the vet felt Hoskins' hindquarters the cat visibly winced. The vet looked up.

"Your cat has been quite badly traumatised by some event. I don't think she has been hit by a car. It is more likely that she has been chased by a dog and grabbed from behind and shaken around. The skin is not broken but there is evidence of some bruising around the hindquarters. Keep her quiet for a few days and feed her plenty and she will be fine. If you have any further problems don't hesitate to phone me."

This story does have a happy ending. After a few days Hoskins was fine and slowly began to regain her confidence. My mother had been quite right. Like her father before her she had come back to reassure us and tell us that all was well with her.

As I write the conclusion of this account Hoskins is sitting on a chair beside me fast asleep. She was born on the last day of the Conservative government in the '90s and has very much perked up since the coalition came to power. She is now thirteen years old and is a fit and active old tory. The dog next door continues to get out and chase sheep, cats and cockerels all round the neighbourhood. If my mother were still alive she would have long ago told it to, "Goo lie down."

The Old People

The village of Brantcombe nestled into the southern flanks of Dartmoor like a piglet feeding from a fat sow. The Church of St Petrock had been without a vicar for over a year when the Revd. John Hay was appointed from Plymouth where he had been a curate for a number of years. The congregation was delighted to welcome this rather weedy young Scot into their ancient church from the rigours of a tough urban parish. He looked very amenable, but they had not reckoned on his quiet but incredibly stubborn nature.

"I reckon he be of the 'igh Church," said Mrs Escott at the Mothers' Union one dark winter evening. "A nice enough parson but 'ee be all about stinks and lace and the Virgin Mary, bless 'im."

Revd. John Hay's induction took place on a stormy winter evening with rags of cloud chased by a savage west wind straight from Cornwall. The wind howled and moaned around the vast church with its granite pillars and moorstone walls while spats of hard rain spattered on the dark high windows. From time to time the lights flickered and dipped while the candles guttered and smoked before recovering and burning straight. The bishop's quiet words were often drowned by sudden gusts which seemed to burst from various dark corners of the church. The congregation was there in force; the more 'low church' members having temporarily overcome their scruples to give their new vicar, or priest in charge as he now was, 'a coat of looking at'.

Life settled down quickly for the new vicar of Brantcombe. He worked very hard from dawn to dusk, visiting, taking services, chairing interminable meetings and faithfully saying his daily offices. Most parishioners considered him a success, his sermons were instructive and entertaining, and above all he was approachable.

One cold evening John Hay was summoned to the home of the senior churchwarden, Simon Sykes. He left the draughty vicarage in his thick burial cloak to walk through the chilled quiet streets of his village. He walked past the corner, past the Tinners' Arms, across the road to the Victorian side of Brantcombe. A train roared past the desolate shuttered signal box and the abandoned platform. Up a slight hill in sight of the moor and John arrived at Simon's gate in front of his comfortable house. He walked over the paving blocks of the drive past a parked BMW and rang the bell at the front door.

"Come on in, Vicar," boomed an imposing voice as a youngish man in tweeds strode towards the front door from the fastness of his sumptuous house. John laid his cloak over a chair and followed his host into his study, a large television booming from an adjacent room. John sat down on a plain chair on the other side of Simon's desk.

"Going quite well, the cure of souls, I think," said Simon peering at John over his half moon glasses. "I've heard good reports, I'm glad to say. Church attendance slightly up, Sunday School coming on well, lots of hard work..."

John felt himself bristle and tried not to let his annoyance show. He felt himself patronised, spoken down to, assessed. He must rise above these hostile feelings and practise the humility that he found came so reluctantly to him.

"I'm glad you think so Simon. Is that why you sent for me, to tell generalities, to give me a progress report? In all humility I have a lot of work still to do before laying my head down tonight."

Feisty little man, thought Simon.

"I'll get straight to the point then," said Simon. "There is one thing that we need to sort out. As a priest are you obliged to say all the offices each and every day?"

"Of course I am. Have I been found wanting in my observance of the offices? I can honestly say that, whatever my failings as a priest and a man, I have never neglected any of the seven daily offices that I have sworn to say."

"Herein lies the problem, John. Surely these days it is not necessary to say seven offices every day. Wouldn't three be enough in the modern world?"

"I made a vow which I am not at liberty to break. Are you objecting to my saying all the offices every day? Surely..."

"It's not what I think that matters, John. The blunt truth is that by insisting in saying all these offices you are upsetting the old people and you do so at your peril. It is not I who am threatening you, but the repercussions of continuing with this course of action are exceedingly serious."

"In that case I will talk to the old people myself. Who are they?"

"No names, no pack drill," replied Simon rather defensively.

"Then I'll bid you good night. I'll let myself out." John stood up abruptly and left, sweeping up his heavy cloak from the hallway.

Next morning, on a day of dirty drizzle, John walked out onto the moor to visit Mrs Narramore in her ancient farmhouse that crouched on the side of a hill beneath a few spindly trees.

"Come on in, Vicar. 'Tis good to see you. Would you take a dish of tay?" she called from her seat by the fire. She was a weatherbeaten, wizened women who had farmed the moor all her life and had retired to a well-earned rest well into her nineties.

"Zit 'ee down by the vire and warm yourself through. 'Tis a dirty day of mizzle out abroad and a good time to keep close."

Five minutes later John sat in the warm with a cup of strong hot tea in his hands listening to the crackle of the fire, the gentle snoring of a tabby cat and the wind roaming aimlessly outside.

"Mrs Narramore, I have been told that by saying all seven offices in church every day that I am offending the old people of the parish. Have you heard anything of this matter?"

Mrs Narramore looked gravely at him through her round glasses.

"There be no old folk alive who would object to your saying of your offices. That's all I may tell you on that subject. Mind you find the strength to continue and trust in God's might to defend you against the forces of the Evil One."

John stayed for another half an hour in Mrs Narramore's snug parlour talking about church matters, but the old lady would not be drawn further on the subject of the offices and the old people.

That evening John felt a certain trepidation when he opened the heavy door of St Petrock's to say vespers. Why he should feel such a sense of hostility in

God's house he could not say but he was determined, with God's help, to continue.

He switched on the sanctuary light and walked up the long nave to the altar rails. The whole church was cold and still. John pulled his burial cloak around him for warmth and glanced around the dark corners and shadowy aisles of the vast church before settling down to say vespers.

As he read aloud the verses and responses he felt a rush of cold air sweep up the nave into the choir and envelop him with a chill breath. He continued with his prayers, but was momentarily distracted by a low muttering and sibilant hissing that seemed to reach him from the shadowy far corners of the church. He could make out no words, but felt first uncomfortable and then angry that someone was going to such lengths to prevent him from saying his office.

He took his time to finish vespers and stood up to confront whoever was trying to disrupt his prayers. The cavernous church was quite empty and John knelt down again to offer prayers for whoever was trying to frighten him.

As he stood up to leave the muttering started again and a low hoarse voice uttered quite clearly the word 'papist'. John walked back through the choir and nave to the door on the south side of the church. He was about to turn out the remote single light that burned in the sanctuary when he saw a faint glow from

74

the blocked north doorway in the opposite side of the church.

"Very clever," he said aloud. "But you'll not scare me, not tonight nor any other night." He turned on his heel, switched off the light and walked out of the now silent church. But the glow continued to shine faintly from the high gothic windows of the south side of the church before fading back into blackness.

Next evening John was prepared for anything. Under his cloak he carried a small bowl, a bottle of holy water and a sprig of box. Before kneeling down to say vespers he poured a little of the water into the bowl and set the box sprig into it on the altar rail. Then he started to recite the office in the shadowy church which echoed his voice back from its dark corners and recesses.

After the first prayer and set of responses the dark muttering began, joined by a droning buzz and some eerie high-pitched squeaks. Despite concentrating hard on his prayers John made out the words 'papist' and 'pride' booming from somewhere in the north aisle. He reached for the sprig as he sensed some force gathering in the body of the church. He had no time to flick the holy water into the choir as strong hands grasped him from behind. Dirty fingers dug into his neck and arms as thin, strong arms dragged him from the altar rails. He had no chance to see his assailants as he was lifted bodily from the altar step and carried roughly down to the nave to the accompaniment of savage grunts and hisses. He felt warm rancid breath on his cheeks and a disgusting smell of decay and rotten flesh enveloped him.

At last he realised that he was in the hands of no mortal force. He began to recite the Paternoster in Latin before a filthy peeling hand was clamped tightly over his mouth. All he could see was a rough oak door slowly opening before him in the north aisle. His last thought as he was borne through the doorway was that it has always been referred to as 'The Devil's Door'. Once outside in the churchyard he was flung to the ground and blows rained down on him from sticks and bony fists. Blood choked his eyes and mouth and he did not feel the hemp rope that was drawn around his neck.

Next morning Mrs Escott and a few of the ladies paused under the tower before going into the church to do the flowers. It was a beautiful clear day without a cloud in the sky for the first time in weeks. Mrs Escott felt a shudder of annoyance as a drop fell from the sky onto her shoulder. She reached to brush it away and her hand came back bright red. She looked up in surprise to see the body of her vicar hanging far above her against the wall of the tower, his black clothes ragged and muddy, with blood dripping slowly from his open mouth.

A School Story

I stamped my frozen feet as I walked up the churchyard path towards the high old church of St Andrew at Harberton. The bulk of the grey church seemed to loom above me against a steel grey sky. A cold east wind moaned down from Somerset to chill the bones and crisp the dead grass that crunched at my feet. I had come to this forbidding place to search out a statue, a monument to a young life cut tragically short. Once again I asked myself why I was making the effort when I could be at home finishing reading my collection of M R James' short stories in front of the spreading heat of a log fire, my curtains drawn against the chill greyness of yet another January day.

It must have been the dream I supposed. The beseeching look on the young man's face would not leave my mind. I must have visited Harberton church many years in the past and remembered the pathetic cracked monument in the north aisle. I had to go back there and visit the place to get the image out of my mind; it recurred like a tune that wouldn't stop playing in my head. A haunting of this sort demanded a confrontation and an exorcism.

Apart from the cavernous and rather austere perpendicular church, Harberton was a nice village, compact and grey, with a splendid old pub opposite the iron gate of the churchyard. The thought of a pint of real ale gave me heart as I approached the huge blank windows and grey slate wall of the church. High in the tower a remote bell struck midday.

Turning my back to the vicious cutting edge of the wind I turned into the porch and grasped the door handle in the semi darkness. The door grated open and I walked into the body of the church, my footsteps echoing from the high grey walls. Frigid draughts whistled through gaps in the high gothic windows. Above and around me rose the pointed arches of the arcades with their carved pillars stark as bones. I paused to read a dim monument high on the wall beside the door which grimly remembered:

Jasper Parrott who expired during a
violent epileptic seizure in the year of
Our Lord 1815.

Not much dignity in death, I thought sourly as I made my way in the dim light to the north end of the dark carved screen with its desecrated saints painted dimly on the panels. The smell of dust and old wax was beginning to irritate my nose. I recoiled as I saw the fragile skeleton of a long-dead bat perched on the slanting windowsill above the Browne tomb.

Reminding myself that this was what I had come to see, I bent over the recumbent figure in the arched niche below me. There lay the slight figure of a mid-Victorian teenaged boy in a short shroud, a wilting lily grasped in his white marble fingers. His face beneath curling hair was bone white and bore a look of resignation that bordered on boredom. His feet stuck upwards at a sharp angle in shoes that had obviously never touched the ground. Carved into the marble slab on which the boy lay was the one word in capital letters: PANCHO.

What was most remarkable about the whole effigy was that a jagged crack ran obliquely across the chest of the figure separating it effectively into two pieces. Yet there was no sign of subsidence in the wall that arched over the monument or in the tiled floor below.

My duty done, I turned for the door, visions of a log fire and real ale in my head. The door scraped open and a tall man came in muffled in an old Army greatcoat.

When my heart had stopped pounding I said, "Good afternoon, Mr Parnell."

"My dear life, you gave I a start! I came to lock up seeing as the day is so raw. I must confess surprise on finding any living soul in here of such a day."

"Can you tell me anything about this monument before we go out again into the cold blow?"

"I reckon I can. Young Pancho was the son and heir of the Browne family who lived over the way at Tristcombe House. Owned hundreds of acres of land and more than half the village they did. They set great store by young Nicholas, for that was his real name. They called him Pancho because his late mother had come from Peru and died of consumption soon after the boy's birth. He was sent away to school and started at Eton when he was thirteen. He showed great promise, but died very suddenly at fourteen. His father was devastated and never fully recovered from his son's death. The Brownes around here are descendants of his half brothers and sisters. Even they will never talk about what happened back in 1871. I bid you a good day for I'm about to lock up and shremmed with the cold."

Back home after the long, cold walk I was determined to find out more. I knew that the family vault lay in the churchyard to the south-east of the church, but was too 'shremmed' to peer down into it on that visit. I determined to go back on a milder day, perhaps when the primroses were showing their shy heads above the rank grass. In the meantime, curiosity demanded some research into the sad fate of Pancho.

If I thought that my visit to the church would put an end to the dreams of Pancho I was sorely mistaken. That very night he came to me in a deep sleep and stood before me at the foot of my bed. His eyed were no longer sightless marble orbs, but were of the deepest blue and full of entreaty.

"The diary!" he beseeched. "Please find the diary..." He then faded back into the darkness, his eyes fixed on mine until he was gone. Now I was duty bound to find out what had happened at Eton in the cold winter of 1871.

Next day I went to the tall Elizabethan House that was Totnes Museum in the Fore Street. The research room was open and I happily paid my £1-25p, made my way up the cramped room and looked on the shelf under 'Harberton'. I found a box file with 'Browne' written on its spine in faded brown ink. Inside was a family tree, some receipts and papers, a will and a tiny diary entirely bound up in waxed string.

I asked permission to untie the string and, having received it, carefully worked on the endless knots that formed a scab up the opening side of the little book. When I eventually opened the diary it was with the sure knowledge that I was the first person to open the pages since 1871.

In a surprisingly mature hand Pancho had written a daily entry. Each page was headed 'Eton' in capitals. The entries began in September 1870.

Settled well into Eton. Today met a boy from Harberton, one Gerald Trist Reynolds. I must confess to not liking him very much and must try to get along with him. He seems to resent my presence here and the fact that I am a member of the other landowning family of Harberton.

October 3rd 1870: Eton.

Reynolds goes out of his way to be beastly to me. I will not sneak on him and will endure his taunts and threats. I think he hates me.

October 7th 1870: Eton.

I seriously think that Reynolds is trying to put an end to me. He hurts me at every available opportunity but hides it from the prefects and the masters. It is becoming intolerable.

The diary continued in this vein with details of abuse and injuries all kept hidden under the prevalent Victorian gentleman's code. I felt increasingly angry with the odious Reynolds who obviously was no gentleman and probably a very nasty little closet pervert in embryo.

The last diary entry was ominously short:

January 19th 1871: Eton.

This evening I am determined to have it out with Reynolds. I don't care what the cost will be but I will put an end to his bullyragging and filthy actions. May God help me in my hour of trial.

The book had obviously been tightly bound after this final entry. The lack of further writing confirmed that Pancho's final meeting with Reynolds must have proved fatal.

There was one more piece of paper in the file, one that I had overlooked. It was the death certificate of Nicholas George Bastard Browne dated January 20th 1871 and signed by Iain Snoddie MD. It stated cause of death as acute appendicitis. On the back of the form was the unusual handwritten note:

The deceased hastened his death by attempting, in his agony, to remove his ruptured appendix with the small penknife that was found grasped in his hand perimortem.

The unspeakably devious Reynolds had concealed his crime well!

One thing remained to be done; I had to visit Harberton church once more. I rode over on my bike on the following Tuesday. Outside the iron gates of the churchyard was parked a small van with 'T. Back, Monumental Masons' on the side. The remote bell in its high tower struck the hour once again as I walked along the gravel path to the porch.

The interior of the church seemed slightly less forbidding as my footsteps echoed from the high walls. Crouched in the corner was a bearded young man with a bucket beside him and a trowel in his hand. He was clearly the mason from T. Back.

"Hello. Your churchwarden reminded me that it was time to repair Pancho," he explained pointing to the recumbent figure in the niche.

The crack was gone. Smooth plaster with a bonding agent had filled it and made Pancho whole again. I straightened up and expressed my approval.

Then something directed my attention to the south aisle on the other side of the church where a small alabaster monument gleamed dully from high on the wall. I read it with quickening interest:

Sacred to the memory of
Major Gerald Trist Harvey Reynolds
who died from the effects of climate
on 19th January 1887 aged 29
at Rajnapoor in India.
'Thy will be done.'

There was one more thing to see. Outside, amongst the leaning slate stones and tufted grass, lay the vault of the Browne family. I could see it from the corner of the church and I walked to it over the uneven grass oblivious to the seeping damp.

It was a white marble monstrosity that reminded me of an entrance to the metro in Paris, a whitened entrance to the underworld with the name Browne chiselled into the top. Down a steep flight of steps, behind rusty gates secured by a massive padlock, lay dim recumbent figures in the gloom of the nether world. I descended the slippery marble steps and peered through the iron bars into the subterranean chamber. Two still marble figures lay on raised slabs. One was a middle aged man of some substance with curly mutton chop whiskers and a finely carved watch chain across his slightly convex marble belly.

The other, lying parallel to his father, and also staring at the vault's ceiling with sightless orbs, was shockingly familiar. It wasn't the shoes angled upwards or the short shroud or the clutched lily that were so startling, it was the jagged crack of obviously recent origin that ran across the chest and stomach of the figure dividing it into two pale and pathetically small pieces.

Roughtor

The farmhouse was at the end of a long, rough track the led due north from the road in the direction of Bodmin Moor. I hoped that the journey would be worth the cost of a new set of shock absorbers for my ageing car. When I saw the house crouching in a slight dip surrounded by stunted and leaning trees I threw all doubt to the north wind and rejoiced that I had finally arrived.

The house was long and low, incredibly old. It seemed to huddle against the wind with its small windows and slated porch. Around it sat farm buildings in various states of dilapidation surrounded by dry stone walls and small fields. I stopped my car in the stony yard near the porch.

"I'm so glad you found us, well done! Come in and have some lunch," called my friend from the door of the shippen. He looked incredibly well and not a day older than the last time I saw him several years ago. He wore filthy corduroy trousers and a ripped check shirt, his dark hair blowing in the strong breeze.

He propped his evil against the granite wall and strode over to shake my hand.

"Country life certainly suits you David; far from the madding crowd."

"There's absolutely no money in it but what with my pension and the occasional job stacking shelves, and with what Jenny makes, we seem to make ends meet most of the time. Tons better than running that bloody gallery in Newlyn any rate."

"There's not much money in being a writer either, I'm afraid, but we do what we can."

David ushered me into the house through the low dark porch, down a passage and into a warm low-ceilinged kitchen where he put an old aluminium kettle onto the range.

"Where's Jenny to? How is she?"

"She's over to Camelford supply teaching this week. She's enjoying it and it pays quite well. She'll be back in a couple of hours. In the meantime, we can have some soup and a yarn and I'll show you over the estate, if you like, after lunch."

"Proper job! I'd like to see your rolling acres."

The farm was a succession of little fields enclosed and sheltered by stone hedges that rose up the hill behind the buildings and away towards the moor on the horizon. Most of the fields were rough grass keep, but a few contained winter wheat that was beginning to grow now that spring was here. A few trees grew in the hedges giving a home to the rooks that surveyed the whole enterprise and constantly commented on the foolishness of farming in the lee of Bodmin Moor.

After a cup of hot strong tea I was shown my room under the roof, up a steep staircase at the back of the house, facing north. It was small, snug and felt remote from the rest of the house. I learned that it had been the female servants' room back in the nineteenth century when the farm employed a number of local people in service.

That night I slept soundly, only roused in my slumbers by the heavy tread of someone climbing the stairs in the middle of the night. Nobody came into my room and I was not disturbed so I rolled over and sank back to sleep. In the morning I asked who had come up to my room so noisily in the wee small hours.

David and Jenny exchanged warning glances before turning to me.

"We didn't think you'd be disturbed so soon. It's Tom Prout, our resident ghost. He doesn't manifest himself to everybody so we hoped that he would leave you alone. You won't see him, only hear him from time to time. He seems to be harmless; although why he clumps up to the female servants' room in hobnail boots when he really should be creeping, we just don't know. We're very sorry that he saw fit to disturb you.

Would you like to sleep in a different room from now on; it can easily be arranged?"

"I wouldn't think of troubling you for a minute. I'm most intrigued and want to find out what Tom's business with me could possibly be. I came here to help out and to find a suitable subject to write about. Maybe I can kill two birds with one stone."

The rest of the day passed pleasantly in making repairs to some of the dry stone walls and in putting the bullocks out to grass. I thought about Tom Prout from time to time, but was in no hurry to find out much about him until I heard from him again.

That night I came bolt awake with the silver moon casting its light straight into my room through the small window. The footsteps seemed to crash onto each stair, firm and regular and increasing in purpose as they thunderously reached the small landing outside my door. I expected the latch to be lifted but a heavy silence lay on the house. Just as I was about to go back to sleep I heard a sibilant whisper from the other side of the door, "Charlotte."

In the morning before the day's work I asked David and Jenny to tell me more about Tom Prout and 'Charlotte'. Jenny looked gravely at me over the breakfast table.

"It's obvious that you don't come from round here. Charlotte Dymond was a very pretty young maid who worked at this farm back into the 1840s. She was the illegitimate daughter of the schoolmistress at Boscastle who threw her out and sent her into service. She was a very attractive girl who had plenty of suitors.

"She had been walking out with Matthew Weekes who also lived and worked on this farm for quite some time. Matthew was an illiterate cripple with a pockmarked face and a drooping mouth, not much of a catch even though he cared deeply for Charlotte. They seemed to be an ill-matched pair, possibly only held together by the force of Matthew's personality.

"Then along came Thomas Prout, handsome, vain and a couple of years older than Matthew. He was related to the widow Peter who owned and ran the farm. One day he came over from Lesnewth looking for a job. He upset Matthew, with whom he had previously quarrelled over some missing bullocks, by saying to him that he would have his job and his girl too.

"One Sunday evening in April, Charlotte and Matthew, dressed in their best clothes, went for a walk. They were seen on the way to Roughtor Ford, about four miles from the farm. Matthew came home alone claiming that Charlotte was continuing on to Blisland where she was to start a new job. When Charlotte didn't return to the farm for her things, Mrs Peter quizzed Matthew about where she was. Matthew became agitated and gave several contradictory answers. After a week men were sent out to search for her because no word from her had been heard at Blisland. A few days later Charlotte's body was found in a depression beside the stream at Roughtor Ford. Her throat had been savagely cut by a blunt knife that was never found. Some of her bloody clothes were found buried in a pit about half a mile away.

"In the meantime, Matthew had done a runner. A police constable, William Bennett, was sent to Plymouth to look for him knowing that he had a sister who lived there. He was found by chance on the Hoe and arrested on the spot. His trial at Bodmin was a rushed affair and he was soon found guilty of Charlotte's murder, jealousy of one Thomas Prout being the motive ascribed to him. He signed an admission of guilt, even though he was unable to read.

"Nearly twenty thousand people came to his hanging at Bodmin Gaol. Matthew had given up all hopes of a fair trial; after an hour and a minute on the gallows his body was cut down and buried under the coal yard of the prison."

"So you reckon that Weekes was innocent? What happened to Prout after the hanging?"

"He lived on in obscurity round here. Those people who suspected him kept quiet because they were afraid of him. He must have died in the end. I hope he wasn't buried in the churchyard at Davidstow where Charlotte's body is buried."

"You really think that Prout did it don't you?"

"Yes, I do. I feel sorry for poor old Matthew who never stood a chance."

I looked at Jenny on the other side of the table and thought, not for the first time, how attractive she was. But I put that straight out of my mind; I was a guest in their house and an old friend. That would have to do.

The day passed pleasantly in wall mending and mucking out. I was good and tired when evening and supper came and I went up the steep stairs to bed on the early side. The story of Charlotte, Matthew and Tom went round and round in my head with a maddening persistence. How maddening that was would strike us all forcibly the very next day.

Once more I woke to hear the regular crash of hobnailed boots on the stairs. The words, "Charlotte, are you ready for me?" were hissed at the top of the stairs and, this time, the latch was violently rattled. But nothing more happened and I fell back to a fitful sleep in which dream images of Jenny in Victorian clothes alternated with Prout's dark features and Matthew's pale, anguished and pockmarked face.

I awoke in the morning feeling disturbed and ill. At the breakfast table I asked if the footsteps on the stairs really were made by Prout.

"Of course," replied David. "Matthew limped badly with his right leg and couldn't have walked up to

Charlotte's room without being noticed. Prout must have timed his visit when everyone except Charlotte was out, perhaps at a temperance revival meeting on the slope of Roughtor."

The day was sultry and unseasonably hot. Clouds of gnats hung in the windless air. Thunderheads rose behind the ragged top of Roughtor, spreading over the sky like vast dark anvils. The pressure dropped as I sweated over the barnyard wall. I was becoming uncontrollably irritable; in fact a red mist was rising before my eyes. I stood up and walked over to where Jenny was sweeping the yard.

Without a word I flung her broom away and grabbed her hard by the neck and one arm. My mind was blank and serene as I heard her gasp: "Tom!" My right hand pulled a sharp pruning knife from my jeans pocket and held it to her throat. From the corner of my eye I saw David running towards me round the corner of the linhay.

"Stop where you are you whoreson bastard!" I shouted. Part of me noticed that it wasn't my voice; it was harsher and sounded Cornish. David froze, his hands at his sides.

I pushed Jenny in front of me away from the farm into a sloping field. "Walk on, you bitch," I heard coming from my mouth. "If I can't have you no man will."

A few minutes later I heard the approaching

wail of a police car. A police helicopter burst with a clatter and a roar from the dark sky behind the looming bulk of Roughtor. I held Jenny tight, ripping the beads from round her slim neck. I knew that my time had come; I must kill her now before a police marksman could draw a bead on me.

I pulled her head back by her long hair. Her neck lay stretched and ready for my knife. Just as I was about to draw the blade into her windpipe and release the gush of her life blood I caught sight of a slight figure walking resolutely towards us from the far corner of the field.

He made no noise as he came towards me through the grass, his blue eyes fixed on mine. I saw that he limped and that his face was pockmarked. The corner of his mouth drooped on the right hand side. He came steadily towards me and held up his right hand. I staggered and let go of Jenny, dropping my knife.

"Hold it right there, sir! Put up your hands and move away from the lady. That's right, sir. No harm will come to you if you do exactly what I say." The policeman was tall against the watery sun.

"Cuff him please, Bennett. He'll cause you no trouble now. All the fight's gone out of him. Pascoe, help the lady. Make sure that she's all right."

I stood in the middle of the field, my arms in the air, not caring whether they shot me or not. The only thing I noticed apart from Jenny's muffled sobs was that Matthew had gone.

Poetry Evening

Spring was here at last. The frost finally retreated before a benign west wind that warmed the cold earth and encouraged the bulbs to burst forth. The warm sun reflected from the austere walls of Sharpham House perched above its rows of vines above the curving river before the Dart plunged around the bend between steep wooded banks on its way to the sea.

As usual I walked down the drive to the house. From the hill known as the tor I looked onto the roof of the old house. Not for the first time I thought over the strange history of the place.

Towards the end of the eighteenth century Philemon Pownoll, Captain in the Royal Navy, having captured the Spanish ship the *Hermione*, was awarded a vast amount of prize money. When he returned to England he bought the Sharpham estate with its run-down Tudor house that he determined to rebuild. He commissioned Taylor, the architect, to design a Palladian villa to occupy a commanding position towards the top of the hill above the river's curve. The house was to be plain on the outside and ornate inside, surrounded by parkland, rich pastures and clumps of woodland. Unfortunately, Pownoll's wife Jane became a widow in 1790 when her husband was killed by a French cannon ball off Calais where he died on the deck of his ship in the arms of the future Admiral Pellew. The house was not to be finished for a number of years after the Pownoll's only daughter ran away to Gretna Green with a man named Bastard.

With my head full of history I walked along the wooded drive which swung round to the front of the house. I looked up at the bullet holes from a raiding German plane and headed for the porch. Time to consider the theme for tonight's poetry meeting, appropriately the War Poets.

I was the first person up the wonderful oval staircase and into the octagonal room at the front of the house. The views from this chamber were amazing: up the river into the woods, up the hill to the trees on the skyline, over the vines to the field on the other side of the river. Birdsong rose from the gardens, remote and sweet. Captain Pownoll's last thoughts as he lay in shattered agony on the deck of his ship must have been profound regret that he would never see his family, house and estate again. I could not shake the sadness of this thought from my head and considered that it totally matched the theme of the evening.

As I stood in the middle of the room I looked

down at the ink stain on the worn carpet. It had been made accidentally by Tagore to his mortification. Today it was revered as an historical relic – way to go Rabindranath! One just couldn't get away from history that night.

I looked up to find the room half full of people who had come in while I was lost in my absorption in the ironies of history. I had even forgotten to take off my shoes. I greeted my friends who sat down quietly on the circle of chairs and sofas.

The evening progressed well; but my thoughts were elsewhere. Kevin read his excellent poem on the American dead of Slapton Sands and someone read a dreadful poem about a dying bugler who seemed to have retained an awful lot of puff. When my turn came I found that I was unable to read the poem about the horrors of the Great War that I had earlier chosen to read. Instead I found myself saying these words:

"This whole house is infused with sadness. Captain Pownoll intended to return to supervise the completion of his plans and enjoy a well-earned retirement surrounded by his family and friends. Advanced in years, he had probably had enough of war and fighting for his country. He had reaped the rewards of war, but the irony of how he earned his fortune came home to him in the form of a random French cannon ball. His widow almost certainly ran through the scene of his return countless times even though she knew that she could never see him again. His last thought was probably of the meeting they would never have. I cannot get these thoughts out of my head; they would be repeated millions of times in houses and hovels all over our land. I'm sorry for the sermon, but this is the bottom line, the ultimate cost of war brought brutally home. I can't go on, I'm sorry..."

I leaned forward to feel hands gently patting me on the back and someone gently hugging me. Then I heard a forthright Devon voice.

"Well said, you've hit the nail on the head. The whole building is a poem, a lament to the folly of war. What you said needed to be said."

I got hold of myself at last. "Thank you Kevin," I said.

With downcast eyes and a few murmurs the other poets filed out and down the curved staircase. Kevin and I sat in silence waiting for the people to go. The sound of the last car disappeared around the curved drive and Kevin and I were left in silence and near darkness.

"I have a feeling that the evening is not quite over," I said to Kevin.

"We are waiting for something I think," Kevin answered.

I wondered why the usual staff had not come up to clear up as they usually did. Then I heard a sigh from the staircase beyond the door of the room. Kevin and I rose without a word and stood quietly in the doorway. We did not have long to wait.

Above us at the top of the oval staircase, just below the dome with its dark panes, a light mist was forming. It swirled and settled into the shape of a woman, indistinct and nebulous, that seemed to come and go.

The figure began to slowly descend the staircase, all the time becoming more solid and real. It was a lady, slim and middle-aged with fine grey hair gathered into a bun behind her slim neck. Her face was radiant as she quickened her pace down the steps toward us. When she was a few yards away I saw that her feet did not move, she appeared to glide down the stairs with no sense of effort. Her presence was not in the least forbidding or frightening; the joy on her face was apparent and infectious. She wore an empire style dress gathered below the bust and flowing to the ankles. I could clearly see that it was of a light grey. She came to within a few yards of us before gliding along the landing to descend the last flight of stairs to the oval hall.

Then we both heard it; the rumble of a coach and the snort of horses on the drive outside the house. The vehicle pulled up at the front door with the crash of iron shod wheels and the creak of leather springs. A door was flung open and someone landed heavily on the gravelled parterre just outside the front door.

The lady had reached the oval hall where she stood expectantly in the centre of the compass rose set into the paving. Her hands rose to her face in a gesture of expectation and anticipation.

The double front doors were flung open and a florid, portly man strode into the hall. He wore a stained Royal Naval uniform: faded blue coat with gold facings and much braid festooned from one shoulder. His grey wig was askew but, such was his joy that he didn't seem to care. He clumped across the flagstones in his sea boots and took his wife in his arms with an easy and happy familiarity, a chuckle of pure happiness escaping from his barrel chest. The pair then appeared to waver and then to gradually fade from our sight.

"It never really happened, you know." Kevin's gruff voice came to me from a great distance even though he was standing beside me.

"I know," I replied, now firmly back in the here and now. "But it should have..."

The Signing

Jason Kellow was having an unusually quiet morning. He sat behind the counter in the shop of the Jamaica Inn in the middle of Bodmin Moor with an unbroken view of the car park through the open double doors. Two or three cars were parked outside; the wide spaces between them emphasised the emptiness of the yards of tarmac that was usually covered by dozens of shiny gasoline chariots. Even the A30 dual carriageway behind and down the hill from the old inn was unusually quiet. About an hour ago the usual monotonous swish of traffic ceased, to be replaced for a minute by the sirens and flashing lights of speeding emergency vehicles coming from the direction of Bodmin.

Jason stared moodily at the large room full of maps, books, clothes and other merchandise that usually sold so well. Opposite him the old inn sign mounted on the wall with a grinning gap-toothed pirate seemed to mock his boredom and frustration. Outside the morning mist was clearing from the slopes of the high tors that lay to the north of the hilltop inn.

With a slow pleasure Jason remembered that he was expecting a visit from Leonard Brown, the ghost story writer. He would be driving down from Devon to deliver a number of his books to the shop and would stop in for the usual yarn and then take his books to sign into the restaurant, sit at a table and, carefully and laboriously sign them, adding the words 'Jamaica Inn' to each copy. He enjoyed Len's company; the man was completely mad, but usually had something outrageous or funny to tell him. He was working on a biography of Donald Rawe the Padstow poet and usually combined his research with a sales visit to the inn. Jason wondered if he had been held up by the trouble on the A30 and hoped that he was not sitting in his overheated car in a line of stalled traffic staring at the smooth remote moorland hills.

A black cat wandered lazily across the car park just outside the shop door. With long black tail swishing he turned his contemptuous yellow eyes and stared unblinkingly at Jason. He held his gaze and seemed to communicate a sense of superiority to Jason, as if to say that sitting for hours in a shop empty of customers was the most stupid occupation that a human being was capable of. Then, with a quick impatient flick of the tail he was off.

The door beside Jason that led to the main part of the inn opened quietly and in came Len with his usual untidy armload of books and invoices. He looked pale and unusually tired but, as usual, greeted Jason like an old friend.

"And how the devil are you?" asked Jason jovially. He waited for the usual reply: "All right down one side" or "Couldn't be worse!" What he got back was: "Oh, fine thanks. A spot of bother on the road, but here I am, as promised, with the books. No price increase despite the horrible price of petrol, so gather ye rosebuds while ye may..."

Len seemed a little distant today. Unusually he must have parked his old car round the front of the inn instead of at the side. He must have needed the loo and put the pile of books down on a table in the meantime.

"You have been overworking Len," said Jason. "You look tired. Perhaps you shouldn't have made the journey today. I could have waited for the books you know."

A slow smile lit Len's pale face. "A promise made is a debt unpaid, and the trail has its own strict laws." Len replied, his eyes not quite focusing on Jason's concerned face.

"Go and have a cup of coffee in the restaurant and take your time signing those books," said Jason signing the invoice and wondering how long Len would be prepared to make his long journey to deliver the books. They were very good, well written, and some of the stories were mercilessly chilling when you didn't expect them to be. They sold well, nearly as well as those of the ultimate 'ghost writer', Daphne du Maurier.

A few minutes later the traffic on the A30 began to flow again and cars began to fill the car park at the side of the old inn. Doors banged and people percolated into the shop filling it at last with life and banter. Jason forgot his friend sitting next door at the table signing books and transferring them from one pile on his left to another on his right.

Jason had just sold a Port Isaac Fisherman's Friends CD to a friendly man from the Midlands with the warning, 'Don't try this at home', when one of the chefs slipped into the shop, a strange look on his face.

"Jason, you know that writer bloke who delivers the ghost story books? He was sitting in the restaurant signing books when I went over to him to say hello. He lifted his head to reply and he didn't seem to have a face. The space between his hair and his chin was blank, no eyes or nose or mouth, just like one of those Amish dolls. I leaned forward to touch him and he started to fade away into nothing. It was horrible..."

A feeling of dread dropped like a stone into Jason's stomach. "Hold on," he said. "It must be some sort of trick. There must be an explanation. Come on..."

The two men left the now empty shop and, almost running in their haste, barged through the door to the restaurant. They rounded the corner to find two neat piles of books on the table, but no Len to be seen. Jason picked up Len's ballpoint pen with 'Holiday Inn' on the barrel and put it back on the table. He saw that one of the books had just been signed 'Len Brown, Jamai...' He picked up the pen again and tried it on the back of his hand. It was obvious that it had not run out and the barrel was still faintly warm.

"You must have had some sort of hallucination, Terry, too much wacky baccy perhaps," suggested Jason.

"You're quite wrong there, I don't even drink," Terry replied.

The two men picked up the books and took them back into the shop. They placed them neatly on the counter.

"I've got it!" said Jason. "Let's replay the surveillance tape." He went over to the screens in the corner and wound back the tape from the restaurant camera. He still had the sick feeling in the pit of his stomach.

The tape clearly showed the table where Len had sat. Books appeared to float into the air from the left hand pile and drop onto the table for a minute while pages turned to the title page. The Holiday Inn pen rose from the table and moved over the page before the book was carefully shut and the pen put down onto the desk again. Then the book floated up to join its fellows on the right hand pile. This process was repeated several times with slight variations of pace and emphasis before being interrupted and stopping halfway through a signing. All through this strange parade of books there was no sign of Len at all.

Both men raised their heads as a car drove at speed towards the shop door. It braked and the driver's door slammed shut as a police sergeant strode into the shop.

"Sergeant Pengelly, Launceston Police Station. I wonder if you can identify this..." He placed a charred book on the counter in front of Jason who knew instantly what he would find inside, on the title page.

"Mr Brown met with a fatal accident near Temple on the A30 about two hours ago. A tractor came out of a side road and hit his car sideways on. He never had a chance and was killed instantly. We recovered this book from the scene of the accident. It appears that he was coming here to make a delivery. I'm afraid I shall have to ask you to come and identify the body. Counselling will be available."

Jason opened the charred book that smelled strongly of petrol. He turned to the title page where he saw clearly written on the stained page:

"A promise made is a debt unpaid
and the trail has its own strict laws."

Robert W Service.

Parent Conference

Working as a teacher in a rural comprehensive school brings some very strange surprises, when one least expects them. An ordinary teaching day, however well prepared, can change suddenly into an experience as weird as anything described by Lovecraft.

One Tuesday I was teaching a large year eleven class the pluperfect tense when Mr Prout the deputy head knocked at the door. The class had been very subdued, their heads were down; each student was still trying to come to terms with the sudden death of Joe Pike's parents in a car crash. Joe's chair was empty; he was a brilliant student, but very challenging on a good day.

Mr Prout beckoned to me with a worried look on his sallow face. It was almost unheard of for anyone, especially senior management, to interrupt a class so I thought that it must have been something important. I gave the class instructions and walked out into the corridor to join Mr Prout.

"Charles, I'm sorry to come into your classroom, especially when the class is working so well. Some parents are asking for a parent conference with you – it's Mr and Mrs Pike!"

"But..."

"I know, but we have to do it. Joe will kick off if we are seen to have done nothing. He is gifted and talented, but his Aspergers will not allow him to forget anything not done. We must help him in his time of loss."

"All right, but how shall we go about doing this? I can't for the life of me see how we can communicate with them."

As I said this I felt remote from all that was going on around me. I could only hear the odd murmur from my classroom. Someone was playing the piano in the depths of the practice rooms and Miss Thobey was clashing hockey sticks with a year ten class. I came back to the land of the living to hear Mr Prout quietly finish his sentence: "...and we'll go as soon as we can. Mr Rowe will take your classes for the rest of the day. I'll give you a few minutes to set work and then I'll take you to see them."

Feeling numb and inadequate I put on my coat and walked across the playground to Mr Prout's car. Soon we were on our way to the edge of town and the rolling acres of Chescombe Cemetery.

Mr Prout parked the car with a deliberation that almost masked his fear and doubt. I got out shakily and together we walked over to an avenue of lime trees that led to a mausoleum at the far end. We passed hundreds of slate and granite stones, some tilted, some straight. The mausoleum lay in shadow; I just couldn't believe what we were, in all seriousness, about to do.

A cold little wind tugged at our coats as we approached the tomb. I felt even more remote than I had back at the school. Whose idea had this been? At best we were going through the motions for the sake of a tragically bereaved Aspergers child, at worst we were talking to the dead.

After what seemed like an age we stood in front of the marble and granite mausoleum. With huge relief I saw a stainless steel padlock on the wrought iron gates of the tomb.

With a jingle Mr Prout produced the key and turned it in the lock. The doors swung smoothly open on recently-oiled hinges and we walked reluctantly in. The gloom cleared to reveal two raised slabs on the clean stone floor. Mr Prout bent over and gently but firmly slid one of the slabs aside. It grated slightly and I boldly slid back the other slab. A blast of musty decay came from the open graves and we looked reluctantly down into the single concrete vault. We could make out two metal coffins in the gloom.

With a sharp intake of breath Mr Prout whispered, "The plates over the faces are open." I could just make out the still shape of a nose and the arches of eyebrows.

"Mr Pike, we're here as requested," said Mr Prout in a small shaky voice.

"Thank you," replied a dusty whisper as the dim frozen lips seemed to move and then, incredibly, "Wait a moment please."

We froze as the metal lids squealed open and the shadowy forms below us seemed to gather themselves to rise slowly into the light. Both parents climbed stiffly out of the vault and stood before it as if to receive us.

It was obvious that Mr and Mrs Pike had been dead for some time. Mrs Pike's chin was more pointed than in life and her nose more pronounced. Her eyes, once a clear and piercing blue, could only be described as dusty. When she moved it was obvious that a number of bones had been broken in the accident and the wounds on the side of her head, so cleverly masked by the undertaker's skill, showed deep and raw. Mr Pike's head had a tendency to loll to the left and his movements were jerky. They had not lost their humanity and I was keen to communicate with them.

"We called this conference," said Mr Pike. "Joe knows nothing of this. Tell him that we are fine and that we are able to watch him for a while. We will not frighten him, we want to reassure him that all is now well. We shall move on; soon there will be nothing left of us here. Before we go we want him to know that he will be all right."

I plucked up my courage and spoke to the shadowy figure beside me. I asked Mrs Pike, whom I had taken to the cinema and a number of dances before she met her husband, "Mrs Pike, Jennifer, have you seen God yet?"

"No we haven't, but we will soon. After that we shall not be allowed any more contact with the living. We must go now, our energy is draining away. Thank you for coming and helping Joe and us. We must go now, but he will believe that you talked to us and that all is well."

With a light dry touch to my shoulder Mr and Mrs Pike climbed slowly back into their tomb. Without thinking we both bent over and quietly shut the metal casket lids. We turned in the confined space of the mausoleum and walked out into the grey afternoon light, closing and locking the iron gates behind us. We drove back to school in silence and sat in Mr Prout's office. His secret was revealed at last; he kept a bottle of whisky in his desk drawer for emergencies, such as our afternoon visit to the cemetery.

When Joe came back to school he looked pale, but determined. Mr Prout summoned me to his office where Joe sat stiffly in a chair.

"We're very sorry for your loss and will take care of you here in any way we can. We can assure you that your parents are fine and that they are in God's hands."

"Thank you Mr Prout. I know they are fine because they came and told me so. They are very grateful to you both for helping us..."

Jan Coo

Beneath the oak trees that gave the river its name the brown waters of the Dart eddied and swirled over the worn granite rocks that impeded its progress to the sea. Under the turbulent brown waters the old river gods lurked and grumbled; things had been very quiet so far this year. They slid round smooth rocks and lay in deep pools waiting for the right moment and brooding about the world that now largely ignored them. If nobody believed in them they might one day cease to exist yet they dare not show themselves in case they were found wanting, ridiculous in their scaly big-mouthed ugliness.

Up on the wooded borders of the moor the river ran swift and deep, its swirling waters the colour of Guinness. The odd tourist dipped his feet in the cold moving waters, but quickly withdrew when the chill reached his bones. Brightly-clad kayakers glided between rocky and wooded banks; their skilled progress was of no use to the river gods. Fishermen were too wary of the dark waters to be of use and swimmers found the swift current and hard rocks too dangerous. So the gods grumbled on, unfulfilled and unrecognised. Perhaps something would happen soon that would be of use to them.

Just above a wide curve of the floodplain Hannaford Farm crouched among its woods. Ancient granite walls turned their backs to the roaring river and faced the few small fields to the north. Gnarled oaks and ashes lay between the farm and the depths of the river which crashed out of its rocky gorge around the bend.

In the hollow farmyard between the thatched longhouse with its deep porch and the low granite barn there were no smart four wheel drive vehicles or black BMWs, just an old Fergie 35 and an ancient Land Rover with a torn canvas cover. Rusty sheets of corrugated iron formed the boundary to the kitchen garden and extensive chicken run. An old man in a gabardine mackintosh with a belt of binder cord stood by the door of the house and scratched his head as a minibus marked 'Duchy College' bumped up the rutted lane into the yard.

When the vehicle ground to a halt a side door slid open and two men emerged to walk carefully across the stony yard towards the bent figure of the farmer who took a few steps forward to welcome them.

"You'm here at last," he said. "You'll find us

all in order. We've cleared out a room for John and there'll be plenty of work here fur'n to do. Us'll feed 'n up and take care of 'n." He turned to a slim young man who stood silently beside his tutor.

"Harry Wonnacott at your service. You must be John Varcoe, here to work on the farm and keep a diary of your work experience."

"That's right Mr Wonnacott, I'm here to learn farming and to work hard. I'm going home to farm in Cornwall when my course is over and I want to learn everything I can."

"That you will, son, us'll see to it. Now come into the kitchen where you will meet my wife who will teach you about the fowls and vegetables. Goodbye Mr Roach, us've got your number if us needs it."

John was taken to the kitchen and given a cup of strong tea, introduced to Mrs Wonnacott, a merry, round woman with a face as crinkled as an old apple. She showed John up to his room above the porch and then took him aside to warn him about the river.

"On no account should you go near the river in the evenings. 'Tidn' safe for man nor beast. Us must respect 'n and never heed its call. Remember this now and mark 'n well. 'Tis the only warning I need give you."

John took this advice to heart and soon settled in to long days of work with a good supper in the evening and a chair at the hearth's corner to write up his diary every evening. He ate and slept well, worked hard and got on well with Mr and Mrs Wonnacott who became fond of him and appreciated his hard work and enquiring mind.

As summer drew to a close the leaves began to turn and the dew turned crispy in the mornings. The harvest was in and the sheep checked for maggot and footrot. It was time to put the few cows into the barn and repair the dry stone walls as well as bring in the bracken for bedding. *Hardly the most modern farming methods*, thought John. In the spring he would be placed on a modern farm owned by the Duchy of Cornwall. In the meantime, John would go back to college and take more exams to complete his course.

He had grown quite muscular in the steep fields of the Wonnacott's farm, had enjoyed the work and the company. The Wonnacotts had two grown-up sons who were not interested in farming; one was a lecturer at Plymouth University, the other had settled in Australia as a mining engineer.

Molly Wonnacott noticed that as the end of John's work experience drew near that he became distracted and a little remote, particularly in the evenings. It had been a wet summer and the roar of the river could be heard behind the thinning foliage of the trees behind the farm. Molly wondered if he had fallen behind with his diary and so asked him to show it to her. He did so willingly and she was impressed by his neat handwriting and with the completeness of his notes and diagrams. Perhaps he wasn't looking forward to returning to college, she thought.

One evening a howling south-westerly gale roared in across the Tamar, ripping the remaining leaves off the bowed trees. Behind the thrashing boughs and flying twigs the river rose and roared across formerly exposed boulders. The whistling wind and shrieking trees combined with the deep plunging and grating of the river rocks to resemble a human voice crying aloud.

John appeared to have gone to bed early; he wasn't in his usual place at the fire corner that evening. Thick curtains were closed against the foul evening; the eldritch shriek of the wind retreated for a while and eventually blew itself out before the morning.

At seven o'clock Molly clumped upstairs to rouse young John for breakfast and a day fixing walls and fences. She knocked on the plank door of John's room, peering round the door to find his bed perfectly made and obviously not slept in. All John's spare clothes were in place, his shoes neatly lined up by the wall. She hurried downstairs to find her husband.

Silently Harry led her outside into the foliage strewn yard. John's wellies had gone as had his notebook. Tracks across the muddy yard led in the direction of the trees and beyond to the banks of the quietening river. Harry paused at the river bank and picked up the sodden remains of John's notebook. The bootprints ended at the swollen river's edge.

"I knew that this would happen," said Harry grimly. "Did you hear the river calling last night? I heard 'n, Jan Coo, Jan Coo, the whole evening long. John heard it too, had done so for a number of evenings before last night. Us couldn't prevent it, it was meant to happen..."

"Now we'll be safe from that damn river for the best part of another year. John was such a nice boy, quite unlike the others, such a pity it had to be him."

"We must report this to the police, the procedure must be followed."

"That's right, just like the other times..."

The river gods in the calming of the turbulent waters chuckled to themselves as they glided round huge rocks of granite to look greedily at the offering the river had finally brought them.

The Bells of St Sylvanus

The coach threaded its ponderous way between thick hedges, down narrow lanes, the driver very conscious that it was out of scale with the lush Cornish countryside. It was full of bell ringers from across the Tamar; the Totnes Deanery annual outing was about to reach its climax with a visit to St Sylvanus and its ring of eight bells renowned throughout the Duchy and beyond.

They had rung at Looe and Liskeard and refreshed themselves with many a Cornish pint on the way. The feeling of suppressed excitement in the coach was palpable; St Sylvanus was the big one, a rare treat to be treasured and talked over in future years. The ringing would be a challenge; teams from away were seldom invited and grudgingly admitted.

At last the coach pulled up in front of some black iron railings in the middle of a long dark village that seemed to have no centre. Small, mean houses crowded along the narrow street which was overhung with drooping branches. Dark windows reflected none of the evening light that had made the fields glow on the long lane from the A38. There was no-one about; the only living thing was a three-legged black cat crossing the road with an unwarranted nonchalance.

A hush fell over the men and women sitting in the coach.

"Where's the church to?" asked a querulous voice from the front of vehicle.

"Down below the railings, m'dear," replied the driver.

Indeed the church lay down a slope below the road, its stubby twin towers hardly reaching the height of the railings. Like many Cornish churches it crouched like a damp toad in a valley hidden from the village above. A steep path zig-zagged down to the door beneath a deep porch. The whole impression was one of remote greyness. Grey slate roofs, ancient grey walls, grey reflections from the plain gothic windows. A few grey slate tombstones had been placed against the steep slate walls of the churchyard.

"Come on then!" said the leader of the ringers, somewhat impatiently. People stirred in their seats as if reluctant to leave the warm coach for the lengthening shadows of the churchyard. They put on coats and sweaters and slowly climbed down from the coach. A small knot of ringers made their way through the arch of the lychgate and down the sloping path which turned abruptly at the level of the church roof.

124

At last the ringers stood below the grey Norman arch of the west front looking up at the unmatched twin towers that rose above it. They started as the massive handle of the west door was rattled impatiently from within. The door swung open and a small man with a disagreeable expression came out into the evening murk. He wore a clerical collar and a burial cloak that was starting to turn green with age. His hair was grey and tumbled untidily almost to his shoulders.

"Come in if you have to. You're late! When you've had your ring make sure you put something in the box for the church restoration. Render unto Caesar, etc. And don't overstay your welcome by keeping me waiting," he said in a high piping voice. He seemed ill at ease, constantly looking back over his shoulder into the darkness of the nave behind him.

One by one the ringers entered the vast dark space of the church in an embarrassed silence. Their eyes gradually adjusted to the dim light of the interior. Large round Norman pillars marched away into the gloom. Dusty rows of chairs could just be seen below the vast gothic arches and the remote heavy roof. The east window seemed far away in the faint light cast by the tall blank windows in the aisles. The white alabaster figures of an elaborate monument seemed to writhe in a crepuscular side chapel.

"Could we have a light on in here please?"

asked the head ringer. A small dim bulb came grudgingly on behind the font. It showed eight bell ropes hanging in a circle beneath the north tower. The parson scuttled out of the west door slamming it to behind him. The echoes reverberated throughout the great enclosed space of St Sylvanus.

The first eight ringers each took a rope and most of the other ringers went outside to escape from the oppressive mood of the church. They agreed among themselves that they would hear the bells better in the open air, a decision that they were to regret.

Under the tower the leader of the ringers called out, "Band to rise". There was a series of ragged peals as the bells were put up, some a lot sooner than others. Somewhat disgruntled the leader called, "Treble's going, she's gone!" and a mismatched peal of sound burst from behind the louvres of the bell tower.

"My God, that's terrible," said one of the ringers from Stoke Gabriel as he stood on the mossy gravel a few yards from the open west door. The round would start off all right, but soon two or three bells would clang together producing a clashing disharmony. It seemed to be getting worse; the clashes resounded and echoed off the blank walls of the rows of cottages in a painful concatenation.

Inside the church the ringers sweated and tried to get it right. They stopped and restarted, called and offered advice, but all to no avail. The leader felt a prickling on the back of his neck and felt that he was being watched from somewhere in the vicinity of the screen. Other ringers felt the darkness gather itself just beyond their vision and advance towards them from the choir.

For the first time in his life the leader swore on holy ground.

"O sod it! We know when we're not wanted! Let's get out of here and onto the coach. There's something not right in here..."

The team brought their bells down in a rising panic. Several of the ringers heard a low growl from halfway up the darkening nave and one or two heard a high-pitched noise like the buzzing of an angry bee. As soon as they could they picked up their coats and made for the open west door.

They stood outside in the shadow of the great Norman doorway feeling shaken and humiliated. The old parson materialised from the shadows and slammed the west door to, locking it with a huge iron key. He seemed pleased with himself, but said nothing to the ringers as he walked away up the steep slope towards the lychgate.

The eight ringers looked up at their colleagues who now stood just below the lychgate. They expected them to move to make way for the bent figure of the grey-haired parson in the burial cloak. Nobody moved and of the parson there was no sign. Somewhere between the church door and the gate he had vanished. Yet at all times he should have remained in plain sight.

Badly shaken the eight ringers made their way up the slope to the gate and the coach looming behind it. As they reached the turn in the path they heard the bells above the empty church ringing up. It was an impeccable performance; there were no words of command from the still interior and no slips. After a momentary pause, a round crashed out in perfect time followed by a number of changes in perfect order. The interior of the church remained dark with no glimmer of a light or sign of human occupation.

After a mad scramble up the hill and through the lychgate, the shaken ringers jumped onto the coach and, having made sure that no-one had been left behind, begged the startled driver to take them straight home. There was no stop at the Pound Arms in the village of St Sylvanus that evening. The coach driver had to admit that the ringing team that had started so badly had suddenly improved. Either that or the possibility that another very similar team had taken over, perhaps an identical team, in fact a 'dead ringer'.

Bodmin, Ohio

Imagine my surprise when one wet and gusty Cornish morning, a long white envelope landed on my damp doormat. Above the address in raised black capitals were the words, 'Pascoe and Wills, Attorneys at Law, 1865 Oak St., Bodmin, Ohio, 44154.' The letter read as follows:

Dear Mr Barnes,

We offer you our sincere condolences on the death of your great uncle Mr Abner H Barnes of 2146 Western Highway, Bodmin, Ohio, 44154.

In his will he left you his property and contents as well as the very generous post mortem settlement on behalf of Norfolk and Western Railroad.

We would appreciate a prompt reply by means of the enclosed envelope to indicate your intentions regarding the property and aforementioned settlement.

We are, in perpetuity, your obedient servants,

James Pascoe, Senior Partner.

I could hardly remember Great Uncle Abner. He had come over to Cornwall once many years ago for a visit. I vaguely remembered a rather quiet man in a plaid shirt trying to keep out the cold in a brisk east wind up on Carn Brea. Although not talkative he was warm and interesting. His father Thomas Barnes had sold a small farm near Indian Queens to Lord Falmouth back in the reign of Queen Victoria. Gradually the small sloping fields with their granite hedges were covered by the sandy waste from a huge china clay pit. Thomas had bought a farm in Ohio which Abner had taken over and worked for a while. In the mid '50s he had sold off the land, kept the farm house and a couple of acres and taken over the town newspaper, the Bodmin Bugle, as owner and editor.

I had lost touch many years ago and so had not heard that he had died. Soon I found out that, at the age of ninety-two, he had been mowing his lawn on his ride-on mower when a large chunk of scrap iron had slid from a passing train and caved in his head in his own back yard. He had died instantly and the railroad had paid a large amount of money very promptly to the estate of the former newspaper editor. And now it was all to be mine.

Like Great Uncle Abner I am a writer, moderately successful, but poor. So I replied in the affirmative to Mr Pascoe, rented out my damp cottage, applied for a US resident's permit and caught the next available flight to Cleveland.

I arrived in Bodmin, Ohio after a long drive south from Cleveland. I found a pleasant small town, not particularly prosperous but modestly thriving, in the rich farmlands of southern Ohio. The land was slightly undulating and open, with distant ridges to the north and east. Oak Street bisected the town with tree-shaded streets running off at right-angles to be, in their turn, bisected by numbered streets that ran parallel to Oak Street. There were two sets of traffic lights hanging from cables at each end of town, a railroad line that curved gently through the centre, grain elevators, a feed store, the usual shops and offices, small churches of various denominations, a municipal cemetery and the newspaper offices.

The office of Pascoe and Wills, Attorneys at Law, lay at one side of the shaded town square opposite the Town Hall and Miller County Courthouse. In the middle of an area of parched grass sat a white painted gazebo with a few old men sitting in its shade. Oak Street with its fine brick buildings with their regular arched windows stretched away to the railroad crossing a few hundred yards away. Katydids buzzed their electric song from the trees in the square and down shaded Oak Street.

My appointment with Mr Pascoe wasn't until two o'clock so I parked my rented car in the shade, remembering to leave the windows cracked open against the heat. I walked slowly in the hot sun to a small restaurant on Oak Street, pulled open the door, went in and sat down at the counter. I was surprised to see pasties in a glass case on the counter, but contented myself with a long cool drink and a sandwich.

Half-an-hour later I stood before the reception desk asking for Mr Pascoe whereupon a stocky square-set man in late middle-age came out of an office and warmly shook my hand. He sat me down by his desk, ordered me a cup of coffee and welcomed me to Bodmin, Ohio.

"I'm very glad to hear that you are thinking of settling here," he said.

"Thank you. Yes, there isn't much for me back home at the moment. I'm researching an ancestor, General Darius Couch, for a book on Cornish soldiers in the Civil War, so this inheritance couldn't have come at a better time for me. My children are grown up and I'm a widower. My wife was killed in a train crash several years ago. I hardly knew Great Uncle Abner and I'm very grateful to him for his generous inheritance."

"I'm very sorry to hear about your wife. I offer you my condolences. You know that Abner, who was a very good friend of mine, was also the victim of a railroad mishap. Norfolk and Western paid a very great deal of money to the estate because he was still editor of the Bodmin Bugle and they wished to avoid adverse publicity. You shall inherit close to a million and a half dollars."

I did not know whether to clap, go blind or go to the bathroom, to use a newly-acquired Americanism. I suddenly felt chilled.

"I'll take you out and show you the property when you've finished your coffee," said Mr Pascoe.

Soon we were standing on the back lawn of my future home in the shade of a cottonwood tree. The former farmhouse was plain clapboard with few embellishments. It had settled slightly on its fieldstone foundation and leaned to port. Beside it was a red-painted barn with 'Chew Mail Pouch Tobacco' in faded white letters on the side facing the road. In front of the house was the dooryard surrounded by shade trees and a short drive to the two lane road. Behind, over an expanse of unmown Bermuda grass, was the railroad, shining high rails which curved towards town after the grade crossing at the property's corner. Only a damp ditch full of frogs and horsetails separated the lawn and the ballasted metals of the N and W.

The town lay a few hundred yards away, an area of dark trees and two or three slender church spires. Behind, in the hazy distance, rose a low ridge with a forested crest. Around the house and its orchard rustled miles of ripening field corn, its tassels turning brown in the hot sun.

Turning to Mr Pascoe I said, "Uncle Abner had a sister I believe."

The lawyer looked suddenly guarded.

"Yes, Margaret died many years ago. Abner made me promise never to tell anyone the circumstances of her death. I must honour my word; I trust you will not think me unfriendly for not explaining to you what happened a long time ago."

"Of course not. I admire a man who can keep a confidence. I will respect his wishes."

Pascoe looked relieved. I liked the man for his friendly, welcoming nature so I would certainly not press the point. With a little research I would find out for myself what exactly had happened.

Mr P. took me the half-mile back to his office where papers were signed and hands shaken. I left with the injunction that if there were anything further that he could possibly do I was to call him without hesitation.

Back at the house I wandered around the well-proportioned rooms. All the furniture had been left in situ and I would use most of it. I chose the back bedroom out of the four available. It looked over the railroad towards town; if I were to be honest, despite the death of my wife at Hatfield, I still loved trains. No doubt Uncle Abner would not share my enthusiasm. I had a lot to thank him for.

In the front room, which faced the yard and the road, I came across a grainy black-and-white framed photograph of a young woman who somewhat resembled Abner. He had never married and I wondered if the picture was of the mysterious Margaret. She looked reclusive and rather hostile. Large, troubled eyes stared directly at the camera from a head that seemed to twist away. The mouth was set in a grim line quite unlike that of her brother's. When I had settled in I had to find out more. I would be discreet because I liked the town and the people I had met; I hoped to settle in the house and shake the dust of the old world from my worn shoes.

I had only been in the house for a short time when I felt a vibration coming from the cellar. The blast of the locomotive's horn broke plaintively on my ear as a train approached the crossing from beyond the orchard. I stepped out of the kitchen door onto the grass letting the screen door clap to behind me as an empty CSX coal train blasted past towards the grade crossing. Two huge blue and grey locomotives roared past with the empty coal hoppers banging thunderously over the crossing, flanges squealing as the train leaned into the long curve through town. I counted over a hundred coal cars, some sprayed with graffiti, before the last one scrawled with the helpful message 'eat shit' winked its flashing red rear end device and the sound of the train faded to distant horn chimes and the clattering of more grade crossings.

I felt slightly guilty as I realised that I would enjoy the passage of the trains. A man must take his pleasures as he can, so I determined to find out as much as I could about American freight trains. There was also research on the late elusive Margaret, my great aunt.

I drove back into town; it was too hot to walk and I needed groceries from the Food Lion. First I would join the town library; I had the deeds to Uncle Abner's house so that would be no problem.

The library was situated in Elm Street at right angles to Oak Street in a Victorian gothic house. I was welcomed by a thin young man with round glasses who issued me with my cards and pointed me in the right direction for the microfiche copies of the Bodmin Bugle. I scanned the columns for a long time to find that a whole chunk from the late 1950s was missing. It was obvious that Uncle Abner did not want the past raked over, especially where it concerned the death of his late sister.

A couple of days later I waited for the merciless heat of the day to cool before finding my way to Harmony Hill Cemetery. It was situated on a knoll on the leafy edge of town overlooking fields of corn and soya beans. Some of the older burials dated from before the Civil War. I soon found Uncle Abner's grave under a tulip tree. The flat granite plaque pulled no punches: 'negligently killed on Friday 13th September 2010' it stated. I saw the firm hand of James Pascoe in this choice of words.

Next to Uncle Abner was an older granite grave marker which read:

In loving memory of
Margaret Amelia Barnes aged 36
died 13th September 1959
Peace at Last

Ignoring the hopefully unintentional double meaning of the inscription I remembered the old photograph of the rather disturbed-looking young woman. I supposed that I should take everyone's kind advice and let her rest. Writers have over-inquisitive minds and often cannot leave matters alone. I had drawn a blank however and probably would never find out what Margaret's fate had been. So I thought at the time; events would soon prove me horribly wrong.

Life settled into a very pleasant routine. I tidied and cleaned the house gradually adapting it to my needs. Soon I was familiar with the trains that passed the house at all times of the day and night. I learned the difference between the whine of Electro Motive Division's engines and the rougher rhythmic chug of General Electric's motors. I usually got a wave from the engineer in his cab; it was only the Norfolk and Western men who were slightly reticent. I learned to distinguish the whistle of the huge auto racks as they passed eastwards empty and the more solid sound of the westward bound loaded cars. I could hear the rhythmic hammer blows of wheels with flat spots worn into them as well as telling a Nathan chime from other engine horns.

The nights were hot and clammy, even with the air conditioner running. I usually fell asleep sometime after the eastbound N and W unit coal train went through just after midnight. I found myself regularly waking at three o'clock for no apparent reason. It was as if I were waiting for something to happen.

One night something did. I came bolt awake at three to hear the screen door to the kitchen slam shut. I know that I had locked the kitchen door, but I went to check it in any case. The screen door was also locked tight so I must have dreamed or imagined it.

Next night the same thing happened; with accompanying footsteps running over the grass towards the railroad. *Kids*, I thought angrily as I went back to my hot and rumpled bed.

As August turned into September the nights shortened by the heat continued like a blanket on the land. I wasn't anxious about my nocturnal visitor, just annoyed at having my night's sleep constantly disturbed. The slamming of the screen door seemed to be getting louder and the whispery footsteps on the grass were beginning to be accompanied by a desperate sobbing. I had a feeling that Friday 13th September might reveal the cause of my disturbed nights.

On that night the heat finally began to break. Lightning flashed in the bellies of dark full clouds and the ridges stood out in stark and momentary relief. The thunder clouds hung low over the ripe fields but no rain came. At two-thirty I sat at my bedroom window with the light off and the curtain pulled back. At three o'clock the screen door smashed shut and I heard a loud sob. A dark figure with bare feet as white as bone emerged to hurry across the dry lawn towards the railroad ditch. I heard the plaintive blast of a Nathan chime from behind the orchard, two short, one long and one short as the train approached the crossing. The figure stopped and glanced up at my window as lightning lit up the whole back yard in white relief. From the long wild hair streaming from its head the figure was female. The eyes searched out mine; they were wide open and quite mad. I knew now with sickening certainty what was about to happen, and what had happened all those long years ago.

The white light gave way to a darkness broken only by the wavering beam of the approaching train. The engine was round-fronted with two slanted cab windows and a long radiator grille down the side. It approached rapidly, the lighted windows of the passenger cars swaying slightly as they rocked over the rail joints.

Another flash of lightning showed Margaret take a wild jump over the ditch onto the ballast, her nightdress trailing into the water. There was a frantic blast of sound from the engine's horn and then the merciful darkness was broken by a shower of sparks from the locomotive's locked wheels. The screaming of tortured metal covered any other sound as the heavy train eventually came to a shuddering rest well beyond the crossing.

The next lightning flash was mercifully short. I could see the engine crew jumping onto the ballast with flashlights in their hands; by then Margaret's truncated remains were scattered over the track on each side of the crossing, an arm here, a leg here, her head resting on the grass with its dead white eyes turned towards my window.

I never told anyone about the events of that night until now. I guess it doesn't matter anymore because the house is no more. I am without a home; when I was away in Pennsylvania a tank train derailed at speed on the grade crossing just outside my house. The ensuing fireball destroyed everything on the property, both engine crews were killed and shattered tank cars lay scattered and piled all over the yard, their trucks dug into my grass and the remains of my orchard.

I had kept my word about Margaret and she had kept her part of the bargain. I had lived in the house for just over a year. Something, or someone, had warned me to be away from the property on Friday September 13th and to this communication from beyond the grave I owe my life.

My friend James Pascoe is determined that the next payout by Norfolk and Western Railroad will be sufficient to build a pretty substantial house on the site of their latest disaster.

Telegraph Hill

As the week progressed I began to dread the journey home for the weekend. It happened every week of the university term; so far my ancient and unreliable motorcycle had performed valiantly and completed the thirty-mile journey to the South Hams and back again early on Monday morning. Autumn was closing in and the evenings becoming dark and menacing. I felt very vulnerable on an underpowered, spluttering machine that struggled to crawl up Telegraph Hill to Haldon's high summit before coasting its smelly and overheated way down towards Newton Abbot. My former sense of adventure was severely challenged on a weekly basis.

On a fine October Friday evening I fired the beast up and set hopefully off into the setting sun. The first few miles south of Exeter were fine; the motor ran its ragged rhythm with hardly a missing stroke. In front of me the Haldon Hills rose towards a dramatically streaked sunset. The sun appeared to sink into the flaming scarlets and yellows of the trees above me making me think of T.S.Eliot's line from 'The Love Song of J Alfred Prufrock':

> *When the evening is spread out against the sky*
> *Like a patient etherized upon a table.*

The bike slowed as the road rose towards the cleft in the hills that was Telegraph Hill. I had passed the white bulk of Lawrence Castle on its crest of hills and tensed as the engine began to labour and misfire. An impatient Range Rover sped by me with an arrogant blast of the horn and something tore loose in the engine causing the bike to wobble alarmingly. It seemed to be giving up, to be heading to the side of the road to die.

It came to the side of the road and, with its dying momentum, I coaxed it onto the grass verge where it spluttered to a stop. There was no chance of starting it up again; I had heard its final death rattle. I left it leaning on the guardrail and stood back to decide what to do. The worst possible thing had happened and here I was beside the rising carriageways, dense larch woods hanging above me on the other side of the road and a drop over sloping fields on the other side of the barrier.

I felt suddenly light-headed and also relieved that what I had dreaded had finally happened. I reckoned that things couldn't get much worse than this. The evening sunlight slanted down between the trees and the sky flamed a deeper red even than the trees. The occasional vehicle swished past uphill to vanish eventually around a distant curve between trees at the summit of the long gradient. I decided that I would set off uphill and phone for help at the petrol station just over the far crest. Being too poor even for a mobile phone I would do the best I could to get home and see to the bike after my return to Exeter where my friends would help me to shift the bike and either fix or scrap it.

It was quite pleasant walking up the grass verge beside the sweeping upward curve of the road. The lightheaded feeling close to euphoria persisted to be gradually replaced by a slight irritation as my outstretched thumb was ignored by passing cars, trucks and vans. I trudged steadily upward in the mellow light of the dying day.

After a few minutes I made out a faint glimmer up ahead where the road curved into a wooded area on both sides. As I approached I made out the flicker of a small fire. A blue van roared past close to my right shoulder and I decided to stop at the fire for a brief rest. I could see that there was someone tending the fire and I was beginning to feel decidedly lonely trudging steadily uphill toward the possibility of eventual help.

Eventually I came to the end of the barrier in the fading evening light. There was an opening between the barrier's end and the wooded hedge that led to the hill's top. On a patch of worn grass leading to a gateway an old man lay on his side beside the fire, his shaggy head propped on his right arm. He wore a filthy grey raincoat with a length of binder cord around his waist. Voluminous trousers were tucked into worn boots. His wispy grey hair hung below a brown felt hat.

The tramp spoke first. "Good evening young fellow. I have watched you coming. Sit down by the fire and tell me about yourself. I have been expecting you; my name is Wilfred. I have been here for some time, ever since my cave in Doublebois was blown up to widen the road."

"Good evening, Sir. My name is Jon and I'm on my way to the petrol station at the top of the hill for help. My bike broke down half-a-mile down the hill. You can just make it out leaning against the barrier back there. I will sit down by the fire for a bit. Thank you very much."

Wilfred's eyes shone from his grimy face. His grey whiskers made me think of a grubby Santa Clause. Even though he had said that he had lived in the gateway for a considerable time since moving up from Cornwall I had to admit that I had never previously noticed him there. His tent was pitched in front of the gate and his piles of logs and twigs lay scattered around the smoky fire.

"They won't help you up at the petrol station I'm afraid. They are very pleasant and helpful, but you and I have a lot in common. I think you'll find that we are both beyond help at this point."

"I'm sorry Wilfred, but I don't quite follow you..."

"Then look back down the hill. Here, borrow my field glasses. There's just enough light to see what is going on."

I stood up as I heard the distant wail of a siren. Through the binoculars I could make out the dim shape of my bike resting against the barrier. An ambulance drew up beside it and a police car pulled up in front. In the flashing blue and red lights I saw men emerge with a stretcher and carry it over to the bike. They bent down and seemed to be examining something on the ground.

"Where is your helmet?" asked Wilfred.

"I must have taken it off and left it by the bike," I replied.

A searchlight on the police car's roof illuminated the scene. I could clearly see two men pick up a still helmeted figure and place it on the stretcher. One arm flopped off the stretcher to be replaced quickly before a blanket was pulled over the body.

Wilfred's form began to waver as the fire started to fade. His blue eyes seemed to bore sympathetically into mine and he said, "You stay with me and I'll take care of you. I'll make sure that you're alright."

The eyes stayed with me as I too began to fade. Relief flooded into me as I realised that my relationship with motorbikes and life had ended.

RAF Davidstow Moor

Autumn in north Cornwall is always spectacular especially when the leaves fly from trees bent nearly double by the wind. The dark and flaming colours of Bodmin Moor and the plateau of fields stretching away northwards to the sea contrast with stormy skies, clouds driven before the wind and rare skies of the deepest blue.

My old friend Stan Darling and I were struggling on bicycles over the northern flanks of Bodmin Moor bound for Wadebridge. Early in the morning we left Launceston on the ridge for Egloskerry then climbed the rising ground towards Hallworthy and Wilsey Down. Deep lanes gave way to open roads on the eastern and northern fringes of the moor. The sun came out as we swooped down the main road from Hallworthy to Davidstow. Stan led as we passed the ruin of a wayside house now full of grass and dead brambles and nettles. We climbed the hill past St David's church with its high moorstone tower and forlorn grave of Charlotte Dymond, the murdered servant girl, in the churchyard. The road sang beneath our tyres and the huge cheese factory could be seen like a vast blockhouse on the horizon. Above the tawny expanse of rising moorland hung the remote rockpiles of Roughtor and Brown Willy.

I called a halt at the top of the hill near the main road and leaned forward to talk to Stan.

"We're close to the old RAF airfield at Davidstow Moor and it's well worth a look. There are two museums in some of the old airfield buildings and we can ride over the whole area and even camp there for the night. It's common land and only the sheep will object."

"Good idea," replied Stan. "My legs are getting tired by all these hills." He came from a flatter part of the country, was very tall and rode his bike rather like a duck. He couldn't pedal with the balls of his feet and so they stuck comically out to the side as he rode up onto the edge of the moor. His determined face was sweaty beneath the brim of his jungle hat.

We turned down a lane between high Cornish hedges, passed the huge cheese factory on our right and arrived at the gate of what was left of the wartime airfield. We paid our modest entrance fee at the guardhouse and locked our bikes to the high chain link fence. Restored buildings lay scattered with a few abandoned nissen huts and concrete barrack blocks behind some old fire engines and another high fence.

We watched a film on the restoration of the buildings and the collection of various aeroplanes and smaller artefacts: old greatcoats, uniforms, weapons, and bits of equipment. Walking into the huts and the former officers' squash court we both had a very clear impression of life in an isolated station far from any large town and many miles from the nearest railway link with home.

"This was the highest airfield in use during the war. It was frequently completely cut off by fog and could be a very lonely place. I wouldn't like to spend a night up here for any money," mentioned our guide, a tall fit man in a red Marlborough cap and camouflage trousers.

I wondered if the remoteness of the place was responsible for the frequent changes of squadron at the airfield during the war. Apart from the RAF there were squadrons from Poland and the USA during the few wartime years the station was in operation. It must have been cold and damp when the mist swirled around the flanks of Roughtor cutting visibility and enclosing the vast airfield so that a lone airman could wander for hours on the moor with no sense of direction or lights to guide him back to his hut.

Somewhat reluctantly our host told us of the fiery collision between two USAAF Flying Fortresses towards the end of the war. It happened in the middle of the night in the fog when both aircraft tried to land on the same runway at the same time. Naturally the sounds of their engines and of their spectacular fate could still be heard on moonlit nights at the right time of the year.

"On just such a night as this do the phantom yanks manifest themselves..." joked Stan in a mock mournful voice.

"Time to make a recce of our campsite," I replied.

We took a cursory look at the smaller museum and rode onto the moor. We crossed a cattle grid and looked across the vast open space that had been RAF Davidstow Moor. It was beginning to seem a bleak place to spend the night even in the warmth of a midsummer evening. There was no village near us; Davidstow was a scatter of odd houses with no centre and, more important, no pub. We would have to make our own amusements on the sheep speckled grass.

We rode over to the skeleton of the control tower near the perimeter road. The concrete building reeked with the sour smell of sheep. Their droppings lay everywhere mixed with crushed fragments of grass. Even the window frames had gone from the tower, the railings that had ringed the high platform had rusted and dropped onto the rank grass below. The remains of the control room resembled a skull with a rising wind blowing shrilly through the socketed gaps. From the top of the tower we could see the remains of the two main runways converging towards the centre of their slightly undulating mile long stretch. Another smaller runway crossed like the horizontal stroke of a huge letter A. The dispersal pans where the aircraft stood ready were lost in a dense conifer forest hard on the flanks of Brown Willy and Roughtor. Long clear avenues through the forest revealed the steeply rising moorland slopes beyond.

Closer to the ruined tower tumbledown concrete huts, most roofless, were dotted around the edge of the airfield. The slots of grass-tufted air raid shelters and ammunition stores caught my attention. Apart from this there was nothing more than the Altarnun road meandering across the moor crossing both runways, its neat drainage ditches and smooth surface contrasting with the cracked and grass grown concrete slabs of the runways and perimeter tracks.

The sour smell of sheep seemed to be growing even more acid as the wind increased from the north. The sun was starting to dip westwards in a fiery orb as the fog began to roll in a dirty blanket down the slopes of Brown Willy to the north. Tendrils had reached the edge of the airfield as we clambered down the echoing stairs of the control tower.

"I suppose we shall have to camp here on the moor rather than find a nice snug farmhouse," remarked Stan, a slightly worried look crossing his face.

"We'd better get the tent up before the fog reaches us," I replied.

We set to and unpacked the flimsy tent and our sleeping bags, wheeled our bikes over the bumpy grass well away from the tower and made camp as the light faded in the damp mist. Soon visibility was down to a few yards and all sense of direction was erased by the creeping grey fog that held us in its dripping thrall. We prepared a hasty supper and crouched in front of the tent on the wet grass to eat it. Soon we were snug in our sleeping bags with the tent flap zipped shut. The silence of the fog shrouded moor was complete, even the sheep were quiet.

Steve woke me in the middle of the night. He was thrashing about, dreaming about an aeroplane.

"Go ahead," he muttered. "Put her down on the main runway. B17, Flying Fortress, incoming, prepare the fire tenders and the ambulances. This one's in bad shape. We'll be lucky to get her down in one piece. Go for it. Here she comes!"

"Calm down Stan, it's a dream. There's no plane out there. Wake up now."

But I was wrong. Through the dark night I could just hear the distant throb of four powerful engines, at least two of which were misfiring. No wonder Stan was dreaming. There was a plane out there in trouble. I wondered how it could land safely in this thick fog with no instructions from the ruined tower.

The stricken plane was coming closer. There was another plane up there coming from the opposite direction. It too sounded as if it were in trouble.

The first plane was now very close, its misfiring engines backfiring almost overhead. With a loud yell Stan jumped out of his sleeping bag, unzipped the tent flaps and ran out into the night.

"Stay here!" I yelled against the roar of the approaching engines. I wondered if the plane was going to hit us but stayed where I was, rooted to the damp ground.

As the plane came down I heard an enormous bang and a squeal of burning rubber as the huge wheel hit the runway a very few feet from the tent. The wing with its two engines roared directly over the tent which thrashed about wildly. The plane roared away down the runway, its howling engines reversing hard to slow it. Then came the explosion as the other plane came down and hit it about halfway down the runway. A blast of heat hit the tent and the night lit up by a vast column of fire that crackled horribly and roared the destruction of both planes. Surely there could have been no survivors.

Then I thought about Stan and a wave of dizziness came over me. I must have passed out still in my sleeping bag. Several hours later I came to with a warm sun on the tent roof and the cheerful sound of birds and sheep in my ears. Stan's rumpled sleeping bag was empty and I wondered if he was all right. Perhaps he had taken his bike and gone for some milk for our early morning brew up.

I crawled out of the tent and looked around. No sign of Stan. Then I saw what had once been his bike. It lay on the weedy concrete of the runway a few feet from the tent, crushed into a curling chunk of metal. On either side of it were thick patches of rubber. Ahead where there should have been a tangled mass of smoking wreckage, wheels, engine blocks and pistons, the empty runway stretched away to the distant horizon.

There was no sign of Stan. I picked up his jungle hat and a few torn scraps of clothing, looked hopelessly around and never found him.

The police were sympathetic, but here I sit in a cell in Wadebridge Police Station awaiting further questioning.

Beati qui Durant

Friday was always the day to go to the pub. It marked the end of the week and a pint on the bench in the porch of the Durant Arms in Ashprington on a summer's evening was a reward for a hard week's work. So we sat with the warmth of the August sun on our faces talking and looking round the square with the tall cross of the war memorial in the centre and the gaunt Georgian rectory looming behind its beech hedge. Summer heat lay on the village like a shroud, there was no breath of wind or relief from the sultry weight of thundery low pressure. The clock in the high church tower struck nine, its dusty notes reaching our tired ears over the shrill conversations of nearby cockerels.

With rapid footsteps Joe came round the memorial obviously heading for the pub. He looked hot and, unusually, was almost running, in an obvious state of agitation.

"What's wrong, Joe? Are you all right?" I asked, worried by his lack of composure.

"Come inside and I'll tell you," he replied glancing back over his shoulder.

We ushered him in through the door to the cool of the bar. As he passed me I could smell fear on him. He ordered a pint and sat shakily down in the corner, his eyes on the door.

"I think I just saw a ghost," he said hesitantly. "I never thought such things existed but there she was, floating about above the road just the other side of the memorial. She was a woman in loose white clothes, almost solid. I could clearly see her bare feet about a foot above the surface of the road as she twisted and turned. Her face was indistinct but she had long hair which seemed to be blown by the wind. But there is no wind, it's hot and sultry. It was horrible. I can't get the sight of her out of my head."

He drained his pint and I ordered another. From the corner a shadowy figure came over and sat down on a chair beside us.

"I couldn't help overhearing what you said," she said. "My name is Susan, I'm staying here to get over the death of my daughter and I can tell you that ghosts simply do not exist." Her voice shook. "I wish to God they did, I'd give anything to see her again..."

We sat in the corner somewhat embarrassed. Joe cleared his throat and said: "I'm sorry to distress you but I know I saw something. I don't know what or who it was but I would rather have not had the experience. We should be careful what we wish for you know."

"I don't want to inflict my tragedy on you. She was killed in a crash by some idiot who was overtaking on the Ilminster bypass. She would have been twenty-three the day after the crash with the whole of her life ahead of her. The driver of the other car was killed too. She was a local girl who made one mistake too many..."

We murmured our condolences and the lady said goodbye and left. She was middle-aged and in no way remarkable. We felt very sorry for her and her presence had put a damper on the evening.

Before the sun went down we walked Joe back up the hill to his cottage at the entrance to Smallwell Lane. We were relieved not to see a girl in diaphanous robes drifting about in the road and wondered just what Joe had seen. My wife felt depressed by the sad story of the lady in the pub and her tragic loss.

Next evening we went down to the pub again to make up for our somewhat spoiled evening. Once again we sat in the hot porch looking out on the dusty square and hoping that the thunderous weather would break at last. This time it was Lynda, the landlady who came out to talk to us with a troubled look on her face.

"You know the lady who lost her daughter?" she began. "She got her wish last night; she woke up to find a woman in her room standing at the bottom of her bed staring at her. The woman had long hair and a sort of gauzy dress. The trouble was that the woman was, in no way, her late daughter. She was frightened, but is convinced that her daughter is trying to get in touch with her. Because of that she's staying another night in the same room. She told me that she feels very bad about interrupting you last night and gave me some money to buy you both a pint. And one for Joe, too, if he plucks up enough courage to come down the hill to the pub one evening."

Our bereaved friend did not come down to the bar so we finished our pints and went home, somewhat intrigued by the developments of the strange story.

That night the weather broke at long last. Heavy thunderheads built up miles high to the west and the pressure dropped still further. Not a breath of wind stirred the dusty leaves of the trees.

Then a low rumble came from the direction of Kingsbridge. A hot wind sprang up and the sky was rent asunder by huge bolts of lightning. Soon huge explosions directly above us echoed from the hills and blasted the whole of the South Hams. It was as if the gods were rolling huge marble bowling balls together in the sky and creating sheets of fire that lit the whole bedroom from skirting board to ceiling. Then the rain came in torrents that poured out of the sky washing the dust into the gutters and flooding the roads and drains.

At last the thunder rolled away in the direction

of Somerset and the rain settled down to a steady hiss. The temperature became bearable and we slept soundly until the sun came up on a saturated world of coolness. The last thought in our minds was how our new friend had fared in the Durant Arms during the night.

Soon after breakfast the phone rang. It was Lynda from the pub.

"I'm so sorry to bother you, but Susan would very much like a word with you before she leaves to go back to Somerset. She was very insistent so I said I would ask you."

We had to go, of course. Lynda sat us down in the corner of the dining room with a cup of coffee and soon Susan came in and sat down with us. In a way she looked relieved if we ignored her extreme pallor and darkly-ringed eyes.

"I'm glad I stayed the extra night because the ghost came back. It happened like this: I had been unable to settle in my room before the storm. A strange restless energy was all around me. I had heard a number of low groans during the day and bottles and cups had fallen off tables on the other side of the room. I even saw a beer glass drift slowly across the bar when there was nobody there.

"After I went to bed the heat was terrible. Although there was no wind the curtain twitched from time to time as if something was trying to get in. I turned off the light and tried to sleep, but found myself tossing and turning in my hot bed. The name 'Tracey' kept coming into my head. Finally I sat up and said out loud: 'Are you trying to contact me Tracey?'

"At this point the lightning started and the thunder began to growl. The curtains parted and someone stepped into the room. When I had the courage to look I saw a pale girl with long hair dressed in a sort of shroud. Her eyes were closed and she stood a few inches above the floor with her hands at her side. In the lightning flash I clearly saw that her face was stitched up in several places and that her eyes were sewn shut.

"Then it came to me: she had been in a terrible accident and the undertakers had done only a token job on her. Her injuries must have been so terrible that the only viewing must have been for identification. I realised that this poor girl must have had something to do with my daughter but could not, for the life of me, think what it could have been.

"Then it hit me. Another huge flash lit up the pathetic figure by my bed and I heard a voice in my head: 'I'm so sorry... Your daughter... Entirely my fault...' Her voice was like a dry whisper that died away. And all the time her pallid lips were closed.

"I brought myself to murmur in the darkness: 'Thank you, go from here to a place of rest. Thank you, Tracey.'

"A great white flash lit up the whole room and the figure smiled. Her dry lips twisted upwards and her eyes opened. She looked at me for a split second with eyes that were crimson, suffused with blood. But her expression was almost human and brought me peace. The thunder crashed and rolled directly overhead and I think I must have passed out. I woke up this morning with a feeling of peace that I have not had for a long time. I'm so glad that I stayed and saw the thing through."

We said our goodbyes and Lynda saw us out. As we stood in the porch with a new day in front of us she pointed up at the inn sign above us.

"'Beati qui Durant' it says up there, 'Blessed are those who endure'. I see a new meaning in the motto. Have a safe journey home; I don't think that any of us shall be hearing from Tracey again."

Lady Sings the Blues

Monday 9th September

Time for a holiday at last! Even though we live in a lovely part of Devon we do need to get away from time to time. A change of scene is necessary even for strangers in paradise.

I have just finished my book on Edgar Allan Poe and the women in his life, and feel flat and washed out. I shouldn't feel like this because it is about to be published with a great fanfare by a major international publisher. I am very fortunate; it was against the odds in the 'current economic climate'. For that read 'people glued to Kindles absorbing anything and everything that was placed on it'. I don't mean to sound cynical but my wife tells me that I am inclined towards gloom. I love cemeteries and was drawn to Poe like a bluebottle to a dung pile.

I miss the company of Poe. He was an entertaining companion, sometimes full on and sometimes as cold as charity. Entirely self-centred, he had all the radiant charm of a neurotic, a charm that could be switched on and off on a whim. He was a wild talent; not always the best poet in the world, but brilliant in the vast scope of his ideas and often in their expression. He wrote the very first detective story in which the application of ratiocination could lead us, with the help of a master detective, to find the culprit. He also invented the theme park, water rides through strange country past natural and man-made marvels. Enough of Poe! But I miss him, damn his eyes!

My wife Rosie said she was glad to get me back. Although not exactly jealous of Edgar she certainly deserved more of my attention than I had been willing to give her for the past few months. Rosie is very understanding; we have only been married for five years. My first wife Wilhelmina died a few years before. She was bipolar and the depths she sank into could never compensate for the highs she occasionally experienced. Like one of Poe's consumptive and often incestuous dream lovers she just faded away to be buried, like Annabel Lee, in a city by the sea. I could do nothing to change what happened and, although I missed her horribly I had to get on with my life. It is hard to believe that I would never again see her ethereal form, her almost transparent skin and her wide, colourless eyes that always seemed to see through and beyond me. I would never hear her voice with its German accent and intonation and her rippling laugh that came so rarely.

Enough of Poe and enough of the past! Rosie and I are going on holiday to many of our favourite places in the Westcountry. We will do the grand tour and see places we both love and show each other places that will amaze us both.

With the cat safely in the cattery at Rattery and the mains water switched off, even though we won't get a frost in September in South Devon, we are ready to set off from our village for over a week of going wherever the whim takes us. First we will head towards Exeter and find a room for the night. A nice snug old pub will do us; a couple of pints and a good plain supper before slumbering between clean sheets in an ancient room below the thatch.

I still feel a sense of loss, however. I miss writing about Poe and I suppose that writing a diary is a form of compensation for an addiction that took me over for nearly two years. Rosie says that I will feel like this for some time and that I mustn't worry about it; soon a new subject will pop up to take the place of Poe. So I must try and be normal and be better company for my patient wife.

We drove out of the village with the Moor in front of us. It was a cloudy day with a few flashes of grudging sunshine from time to time. We decided to drive up onto the Moor and have lunch in Widecombe before turning east to Exeter. The heather would be out on the flanks of the tors and the clouds would be spectacular.

Once clear of the A38 we drove up steepening lanes to emerge onto open moorland near Cold East Cross. Under a clearing sky we could see the blue haze of South Devon with its woods, fields and occasional glinting towns below us. We could even see the faint line of the Channel somewhere behind Teignmouth. The air was clean as we parked beside a pile of granite with a view of Rippon Tor and Hay Tor behind it. I rolled down the window and Rosie absently leaned forward to turn on the radio.

"What on earth are you doing?" I snapped before apologising and making the excuse that I was still wound far too tight. "I'm so sorry to have done that. It was very stupid of..."

I stopped suddenly when I heard the low, delicious voice of a black singer. I don't think I had ever heard anything so beautiful, so captivating. Rosie went to switch off the radio.

"Wait," I said. "Please..."

The words came slow and clear across the years. It was obvious that the song had been recorded sometime in the '30s or '40s; the use of muted trumpets was a giveaway. But it was the languid voice and the words that held my attention.

*Little white flowers will never
awaken you,*

*Not where the black coach of sorrow
has taken you...*

"James!" said Rosie sharply. "Come back, you're miles away." She switched off the radio and I turned to her.

"What's that song called?" I asked.

"I can't seem to remember. 'Ruby Tuesday' or 'Thank God it's Friday', or something like that. And I think it was Ella Fitzgerald who recorded it sometime during the '40s in America. I've heard it before but can never seem to grasp all the words."

"It certainly had a hypnotic quality, a bit like Poe at his gloomy best..."

"James, we came here to get away from Poe and the lost Lenore. Why was he so obsessed with fabric softeners anyway?"

The spell broken, we laughed together and drove on to Widecombe. Although the weather was clearing the song had cast a shadow over the day. It was not an unpleasant shadow but it made concentrating on the here and now more difficult than it already had been.

We found a cosy room at the New Inn in Widecombe and fell asleep as the bell boomed eleven o'clock from the high granite tower of St Pancras' church just across the road.

Tuesday 10th September

A good night's sleep, although I had a curious dream. There was a woman in it, pale, ethereal but always just out of view in the fastnesses of the Moor. Overwork, I suppose. After a good breakfast and a walk round the churchyard we lifted our eyes to the hills where Bonehill Rocks crouched above us a couple of miles away. The distant cries of sheep and the occasional deep croak of ravens followed us back to the car.

"Exeter," I said and we drove away from Widecombe's cluster of houses around its imposing church, up the long hill south, turning off to pass Hay Tor gaping like a broken tooth at the blue land spread below.

We arrived in Exeter and checked in at Endicott's Hotel in South Street. After coffee in the low-beamed dining room we walked towards the cathedral. The crooked little church of St Martin's in a corner of Cathedral Close drew us in and we sat in a narrow pew looking at the ornate monuments with their marble skulls. The wailing note of a saxophone came through the open door in waves, intruding above the clatter of traffic from the High Street and the conversations of the people walking along the Close.

Suddenly I stiffened in my pew. The music was louder, languid but more obtrusive. The notes came with an inevitability that seemed over- familiar. As the saxophone seemed to sob to the end of the song Rosie rushed out of the narrow church into the sunlit close. Shakily I followed her to find her deep in conversation with the musician, a short man in a tattered dinner jacket. I waited to the side to let her finish. She dropped some coins into the busker's hat and walked over to me.

"Let's have a drink," she said. We went a few paces into a crowded pub called the Well House that had a good view over the grass lawns to the cathedral. She ordered and we looked round for somewhere to sit. The languid tune was still drifting round my head as we went down a spiral staircase into the empty cellar that was ancient and contained the well for which the pub was named. There, in a glass-walled niche in the rough stone wall, lay a dusty human skeleton.

"I was wrong," said Rosie, "about that song. It was not recorded by Ella Fitzgerald at all. Billie Holiday sang it in 1941 against the wishes of most people. Apparently the song has a dark reputation. It was composed in Hungary in the early '30s and became known as the 'Hungarian Suicide Song'. The BBC and other broadcasters banned it for years and it's actually called *Gloomy Sunday*."

Still staring at the bony figure in the wall I replied, "It is rather lovely in its way but it gets inside your head in an insidious way. I don't really want to hear it again for a long time."

I still felt shaken and, staring at the small skeleton, I had a vision of my late wife in her crypt, by now in a very similar condition to the collection of ancient bones in the wall. I shuddered and stood up. The cellar walls seemed to be closing in on us and I needed the sunlight and even the raucous sound of the lone saxophone player on the cobbles in front of the cathedral green. So we went, leaving our glasses half full on the raised capping stones of the well. In my head I heard my voice saying, "Good night, Wilhelmina."

"Let's head west," I said. "We can be in Cornwall in around forty minutes if we take the A30, and stay the night in Launceston."

"Good idea," agreed Rosie. "We could do with a breath of Cornish air. You need to unwind and shake Poe from your bones."

"An unhappy choice of words if I may say so," I added.

Soon we were off through the suburbs of Exeter and onto the A30 at Ide. We drove beneath the frowning ridge of Haldon with its white tower and were soon well to the north of the Moor. High tors rose above us on the remote flanks of tawny Dartmoor between Okehampton and the Tamar. Soon we came to a downward slope and crossed the river into Cornwall. Rosie absentmindedly went to switch on the radio, but I stopped her. The plaintive tune of *Gloomy Sunday* was still in my head and I wanted desperately to forget it, to leave it safely back in Devon.

Launceston was a delight with its stump of a castle on its hill and its grey-roofed jumble of buildings clustered below in winding streets that followed the contours of the mound. We found a good room at the Eagle House Hotel with a wonderful view over the vale of the Kensey to the west. After a good supper we watched the sun go down behind the wooded ridge beyond St Stephen's church. Bats flitted about in the sun's afterglow as we set out to walk in the warm dusk up the hill from the hotel to the castle gateway and the open castle green beyond. I still couldn't get that damned melody out of my head.

A few couples strolled over the grass in the dusk. The moon was rising as I saw the pale figure of a woman on her own against the dark wall of the gatehouse that led down to the Town Hall. There was something familiar about the woman even though distance blurred the illusion. Surely it couldn't have been Wilhelmina who had been in her grave this past six years? Rosie had never met her; I must have been imagining things because of my over exposure to Poe and my nervous exhaustion after completing the book.

173

That night I dreamed once again of my late wife. But she was just a bag of bones; the smile on her wasted face held no expression, no welcome or warmth. Her bony hand on mine was light and dry, hardly there at all.

Wednesday 11th September

I awoke curiously tired and sat on the edge of the bed trying to feel normal. Rosie persuaded me to come and have some breakfast and then I felt more myself. At least I had forgotten the tune of that damned blues song.

We walked around Launceston admiring the views over the surrounding countryside. As the church clock struck ten and the little black quarterjacks in the town Hall clock struck their tinny bell we climbed up to the top of the massive ruined tower of the castle. Perched safely at the very top under the flagpole we could see all the way west to Bodmin Moor with its sharp rockpiles of Roughtor and Brown Willy. Back to the east across the Tamar rose the commanding heights of Dartmoor with the occasional tor highlighted against the sky. With the sun on it the remote slopes looked like the Scottish Highlands.

We were still in the gloom of an overcast morning. Suddenly, floating up on a damp breeze, came the bold sound of a trumpet from some dusty attic far below. It was playing *Carnival in Venice* with considerable skill and aplomb. Then it stopped and, from the plaintive opening notes I recognised *Gloomy Sunday* once again. My heart missed a beat and I thought of the tedium of the tune running through my head for the next few hours.

"James," said Rosie at my side. "You've tensed up again. Is it that tune?"

"Yes," I said between clenched teeth. "Let's lay this to rest and go to the library and find out as much as we can about it. Total immersion is the answer."

So we did. We sat in the modern, spacious and well-lit room and fired up Google. What we found out didn't really solve anything, but we left the library much wiser.

The song was composed by Rezso Seress, a Hungarian, in Paris in late 1932, and the lyrics written by Laszlo Javor. It was first recorded in Hungary in 1936, at a time of increasing despair caused by rising unemployment and the growth of fascism. It captured the mood of the times, elevating the personal to the universal. The first recording in English was by Hal Kemp in 1936 with English words by Sam M Lewis. The most popular version of the song was recorded by Billie Holiday in 1941.

The song became famous for being associated with suicides all over the world. If a song can be called haunted this one was. In fact Seress himself committed suicide in 1968. It took him two attempts; throwing himself out of a window in Budapest did not finish him so he strangled himself in hospital with a piece of wire.

Cheerful stuff. Lunch in the old Liberal Club near the church tower would cheer us up so up we went into the light and airy room with its oblique view of the castle above and direct sight of the Victorian Methodist church across the road. Lunch was delicious and restored our flagging spirits.

Rosie looked mischievously over the table at me.

"I wonder if this building was designed by Sylvanus Trevail. He was a famous Cornish architect who blew his brains out in the women's toilet on a Great Western Railway train just out of Bodmin Road Station," she said.

"I'm glad to say it wasn't," replied a rather stern Cornish voice from behind us. "It was designed by our own Otho Peter."

Put firmly back in our places we listened to the piano at the other end of the room. We enjoyed a wistful version of *As time goes by* and clapped enthusiastically at the end. Then the now familiar haunting notes of *Gloomy Sunday* dropped like wet sliding leaves on our ears. It was almost unbearably lovely, but nobody clapped when the last notes faded. Then an embarrassed flurry of uneven clapping self-consciously broke out as if nobody wanted to admit that they had been moved by the music.

I sat in a sweat. Rosie reached a hand over and said: "There's something lovely and dangerous about that song. It makes me think of a vault with a way in, but no way out."

"That's a very good way to put it," I replied. "It's like sweet flowers that are going over. Analysing it makes it easier to live with. I think I'll be all right now."

We left Launceston in the afternoon on our way to Boscastle where we found a snug bed and breakfast hard by the harbour. We strolled in the deep shadow cast by the high hills on either side of the stream that led to the harbour. Both of us remembered the huge flood that tore down the narrow Valency Valley a few short years ago sweeping cars and vans out to sea in a roaring torrent that swept away the sides of houses and ripped the heart out of the village. Huge trees were jammed under the bridge further damming the rivers; the grinding of tortured rocks must have been deafening.

I looked in the window of the Witchcraft Museum and was tempted to go in. An old grey-haired lady standing by the door looked at me intensely and said, "You don't want to go in there today m'dear. You'm troubled by something not of this world and 'twould be a dangerous mistake to go in. I'll not sell you a ticket today if you'll forgive me."

"Thank you," I found myself saying. "I'm sure you're right. Another day perhaps."

Seconds later I found myself drawn to look over the channelled stream of the narrow river to the opposite bank where stood a pale, familiar figure whose face I couldn't see. The few walkers were stepping round her, but didn't seem to notice her. I knew that she was there for me, but it seemed strange that Rosie had not seen her. Perhaps she was just a figment of my strained imagination.

That night we slept well if you discount the vivid dream I had. In it my late wife lay in her coffin. She was no longer a bag of bones but a shrivelled corpse in the late stages of decomposition. She was grey and almost unrecognisable as a human being, but I knew her even in her changed state. I awoke in the morning drawn and puffy around the eyes. Thank heavens dreams are recognisable as such.

Thursday 12th September

Boscastle had become oppressive and enclosing with its steep valley sides and violent history so we left just after breakfast. We decided to go to Truro, a bright and cheerful city full of promise and light.

Having wound through interminable twisting lanes in a wind-blasted landscape we came, at last, to the A39 at Davidstow. The car radio remained resolutely switched off and the wind hissed across the denuded landscape.

"Hang on," I said. "There's an old airfield just up the road that I'd like to see."

We turned off and passed the enormous cheese factory beside the scattered huts of the airfield. Rattling over a cattle grid we were suddenly no longer enclosed by banks. A vast sheep-haunted plain stretched away to some dark conifer plantations below the flanks of Bodmin Moor. The narrow road crossed the remains of vast concrete runways that sprouted clumps of coarse grass in the cracks of the decaying concrete. Half-a-mile away the remains of the control tower rose stark against the sky, glassless windows like eye sockets in the blast of the wind.

On the far side of the airfield were a few huts and a couple of hangars. A windsock indicated the possibility of some flying activity. Some light planes sat tethered to steel staples in the concrete. As we approached we also saw signs of human activity; a group of men in RAF uniform were standing around holding musical instruments under a banner advertising the annual RAF Davidstow Moor Air Day in October.

At a command from the bandmaster the musicians formed up into marching ranks, the wind flapping the skirts of their greatcoats round their legs. I stopped the car and wound down the window as faint strains of *The Dambusters March* carried on the wind.

"They are wearing World War II uniforms, you know," Rosie told me.

After a pause the band struck up Glenn Miller's *In the Mood* and then...

After a few notes of the introduction I realised, with a start, that once more we were hearing the rising cadences of *Gloomy Sunday* brought to us by the surging wind. At times the sound seemed far away, at others buffeted close. The falling cadences brought the song to an end and I was actually sorry that it had finished.

As I drove back across the airfield I remarked that I was getting used to the song and that it didn't frighten me anymore. My heart was thumping in my chest but I felt strangely exhilarated by hearing the song once more. It didn't occur to me then that this acceptance was a dangerous sign; I was relieved that I was no longer alarmed by the haunting song.

But I did feel tired so we stopped by the cattle grid for a minute so that I could have a brief nap before resuming our westward journey. Sitting in the driver's seat I drifted off for a minute to find myself in a familiar vault kneeling before the open coffin that held the remains of Wilhelmina.

It was obvious that she had been dead for some time. The decay was not markedly advanced although the pallor and shrunken features made a parody of my late wife. The eyes opened and colourless eyes looked at me with a spark of life. The thin lips twisted and I woke up with a start.

"Goodness," said Rosie. "You must have had a bad dream."

"You could say that," I shuddered.

Soon we were speeding westward on the Atlantic Highway, through Camelford to Wadebridge and down to grey granite Bodmin where we stopped at the old prison for lunch.

The granite bulk of the prison dominated one side of the town. Most of it was roofless. Jackdaws hopped and fluttered on the chimneystacks and grass-grown fragments of roof and numerous barred windows punctuated rearing walls. A deliciously grim place with the only surviving example of a gallows with its brick pit beneath.

In one of the damp cells was an exhibition about the unfortunate Selina Wadge who was executed in the 1870s for infanticide. She was not hanged in the execution shed but from a window above the alley where bicycles are now parked. A faded photograph of Selina was mounted on the wall; her bleached out features were oddly attractive. I realised that her mad eyes were Wilhelmina's.

Strange how I was beginning to accept the formerly unacceptable. Without mentioning it to Rosie, who was absorbed in the history of the savage murder of the great-grandfather of Nevil Shute, I thought quite calmly that the reoccurrence of *Gloomy Sunday* was deliberate, that Wilhelmina seemed to be getting closer and that I was beginning to acknowledge the impossible. Nothing to worry about however; a writer's mind invariably forms patterns where they do not normally exist. I was in no danger so long as I regarded these occurrences as echoes, the reaction of a tired mind to the strains that it had been constantly subjected to for far too long. Now that these strains had been lifted shreds of tension clung on despite a change of pace and scene.

We decided not to visit the Shire Hall in Bodmin to witness a re-enaction of the trial of Matthew Weeks for the murder of Charlotte Dymond on the moor's edge in 1844. Poor Matthew was found guilty after being forced to sign a confession he could not read. He was unable to speak in his own defence and was duly hanged at Bodmin Gaol. Job done! Forty thousand Cornishmen enjoyed the spectacle of the hanging and the matter was laid to rest.

On we went towards Truro on the A30, Kernow's spinal column. We missed the turning south to Truro and stopped for a picnic lunch at a lay by on high ground with a view over to distant Carn Brea ridge behind Redruth. As we ate our sandwiches in the windy lay by, I noticed the name on a sign. I always look out for 'Mrs Baggit' signs, put up in the '70s and showing some Sal Scratch advising us to take our litter home. This sign said 'Chybucca', a name I found ominous.

"What does that mean?" Rosie asked.

"'House of ghosts' in Cornish," I replied. "Obviously there was a haunted house around here at one time. But not now; I can't see any buildings up here for a long way."

Maybe it was the power of suggestion on my susceptible mind, but I saw a woman standing in a gateway on the other side of the road. Her long fair hair blew in the wind and a slight smile played on her pale lips. Wilhelmina! A large Ginster's truck swung past and the gateway was empty. *Up from Cornwall daily*, I thought ironically.

We arrived in Truro in the middle of the afternoon and found a small hotel near the town centre. After a walk around Boscawen Street we went into the cathedral to sit down away from the traffic and hard granite pavements. The organist was practising for the Sunday service; music thundered and echoed around the cathedral. We sat not far from the main doors enjoying the sunlight slanting through the stained glass windows.

One window in particular caught our attention. The large east window above the main altar contained a deep blue piece towards the centre.

"Did you know that the blue piece was put there during the war as a temporary repair after a boy fired a rifle out of a window and broke the east window?" said Rosie brightly. At that point a horrible new factor entered the equation. I knew that I wanted to kill my wife, my dear companion and lover Rosie who had always been so good to me. I had to keep it a secret from her and realise that it was just one more weird aberration in a string of strange occurrences. One more echo from the past, an inappropriate thought that one tries out for size and then rejects as ridiculous.

I took her hand as we sat there in the vast church. The organ music stopped at last, the echoes dying out from the walls' multitude of surfaces. Then the quiet, creeping, spooky introduction to *Gloomy Sunday*, played, no doubt, as a joke.

The arrangement was very good and made me think of a waltz, swooping cadences that seemed to sway and writhe in the enclosed space of the vaulted cathedral. I was glad to hear it again, was no longer afraid or uneasy. When it finished I turned to Rosie and said: "There, that wasn't so bad, was it?"

"Rather good, actually. They're playing our song," she replied.

A dark rage came over me. No! It wasn't 'our song' at all! It was Wilhelmina's song to the exclusion of everyone else. I tried not to show my intense irritation, but I sat there tense in the middle of the empty space. If Rosie realised how I was feeling she did not show it. I realised that was the answer. Carry on as normal and life will revert to what it should be.

Sleeping was difficult that warm night. When I did finally drop off I soon found myself in the vault by the sea with Wilhelmina's body. It had changed again and showed no sign of decay at all. Her face was pale and held no expression.

Once again her eyes were open and showed a flicker of recognition. She smiled at me and raised her right hand to weakly beckon to me. At that point I mercifully woke up to hear Rosie's light snores beside me. I found myself picking up a pillow to smother the noise and stopped myself before covering her head. I lay awake for the rest of the night thoroughly alarmed by what had almost happened as I left my dream state. This would not do, I must get a grip on this situation before I lose what's left of my mind. I dreaded what Friday would bring.

Friday 13th September

I struggled awake on the Friday morning feeling worse than ever. Rosie looked at me in a pitying way and gently suggested that we go down to breakfast. How could I even think of doing away with such a loving person? I must get a grip on this situation and control my overwrought imagination if I am to move forward to normality.

The radio was on at breakfast and, inevitably, played the Billie Holiday version of *Gloomy Sunday* with its swooping muted trumpet introduction. That set the mood for the morning. Try as I might I remained silent and withdrawn, trying constantly not to snap at my loving wife who seemed to be going out of her way to do everything to irritate me.

After coffee I finally got hold of my dark mood and somehow banished it. I became a much nicer person and we both enjoyed browsing in the bookshops and our 'elevenses' in Charlotte's Tea Room. The view up cobbled Boscawen Street was wonderful and the statue of the soldier from the Duke of Cornwall's Light Infantry quite amazing. It was only when you saw the number of names of the fallen that you realised what the First World War was all about.

We decided to head for West Penwith with its rugged interior and strange island light. This is where Cornwall gathers its forces to resist the huge Atlantic rollers and shows the world its true strength. *Blessed are those who endure*, I thought, remembering the motto on the sign of our village pub. If I too could endure then everything would work out, everything would be all right.

We drove up the hill out of prosperous Truro, passed the hospital and headed for mining country. The land became progressively poorer, little stone walled fields, badly drained with sedge and yellow grass. Outcrops of granite showed themselves from time to time as we approached the A30 which would take us past Redruth and Camborne and its industrial wastelands.

Once past the gaunt mining chimneys and ruined engine houses the land became greener and more pleasant. At last we came close to Mounts Bay and the steep castled island of St Michael's Mount. We drove through scattered villages and came to the coastal plain near Penzance. We parked in Penzance off Market Jew Street and bought pasties for lunch. Sitting on the harbour wall we heard a tremendous roar and looked up to see the helicopter pass over us on its way to the Isles of Scilly.

At last I was feeling really good. I had overcome my bad mood and obsession with death and found it hard to believe that I had felt so murderously evil. Then Rosie dropped the end of her pasty into the harbour.

"Oops," she said crossly. "I was enjoying that. Well, it is Friday 13th today."

"Bad luck," I replied thinking how we had managed to overcome superstitious fears.

Behind us there was the screech of brakes and a sharp high scream. We turned round to see a car half on the pavement and a woman lying in the gutter with blood gushing from her open mouth. I saw, with a profound shock, that it was Wilhelmina.

I momentarily lost sight of her as a policeman bent over her to give her assistance. The driver of the car, a young man, sat on the kerb with his head in his hands and, soon enough, we heard the wail of an ambulance approaching at speed. Then things happened very fast. The policeman shook his head as the ambulance crew approached at a run. They bent over the still figure in the gutter doing the tests to see if any life remained. The woman was obviously dead. She was gently placed on a stretcher, covered and taken away in the ambulance.

Before her face was covered I saw, with a shock, that her hair was black and that her open eyes were brown. I must have imagined that she had been Wilhelmina. I felt devastated that a life had been lost in so random a manner.

We walked silently up a slipway past Holman's dry dock. Chapel Street led us to the church of St Charles King and Martyr where we sat in the sub tropical churchyard under a palm tree. No-one was playing *Gloomy Sunday* which was just as well for both of us.

We left Penzance under a cloud past rows of council houses. The land rose to granite uplands, distant rounded hills with a few houses scattered about in their lee.

"Let's stay the night in St Buryan," said Rosie.

"Good idea," I agreed.

The road dipped several times into remote valleys before we came to the plateau that finished at Lands End. The village of St Buryan surrounded its church with some ancient houses that seemed to crouch out of the wind behind stone hedges. Other more modern houses made up the compact village. The pub in the village centre had a room and a warm welcome for us. The landlord was rather subdued and told us that one of the villagers, Mrs Hoskins, had been killed earlier in the day by a car near the harbour in Penzance. She had worked part-time at the pub and would be badly missed by everyone.

Our room was comfortable with a good view westwards towards Lands End which was just a handful of miles down the road. Supper was excellent and the two pints of Doom Bar helped to restore a feeling of normality to the situation. There was a jukebox in the corner with some old favourites on offer. I got up to look at it and chose the obvious choice, Billie Holiday's version of *Gloomy Sunday*.

Before it started Rosie remarked that I was becoming addicted to the song. I replied that it was better than being afraid of it and startled every time we heard it. Then the brief, muffled introduction glided down the scale and the beautiful grave voice sang the familiar words with perfect clarity. I had come to terms with the song now all I had to do was come to terms with the 'echoes', the dreams, the sightings and the murderous feelings against my wife. None of them was real; each was the result of an over-stimulated imagination and years of repression. I could explain none of this to Rosie; although she knew that something was wrong it would not have been fair to frighten her with my morbid nonsense.

A final stroll round the village looking at the church and some of the old buildings was delightful. We saw the old corner shop where poor Julie Christie was horribly raped in Pekinpah's film *Straw Dogs* and learned from an old farmer that the church tower at St Buryan could be seen from the islands on a clear day. He also told us that the ancient kingdom of Lyonesse which lay between Lands End and the Scillies had been submerged centuries ago and that, on a clear night, you could hear the muffled ringing of church bells from beneath the sea.

"And the merrymaids sit on the rocks and comb their hair in the moonlight," added Rosie later when the farmer had walked away down a lane.

We went to bed early with every prospect of a good night's sleep and woke up on Saturday morning without dreaming at all. The sun was out and the curse had lifted.

Saturday 14th September

A good breakfast at the Hawkins Arms and we set out to walk part of the Coastal Path. We carried pasties, sandwiches, water and a first aid kit in a rucksack.

Through an open gateway we saw a circle of standing stones in a field and went to look at them. They were called the 'Nine Maidens' and had apparently been turned to stone for daring to dance on a Sunday.

"*Gloomy Sunday* seems to be the normal state of affairs round here," I said to Rosie.

"Aaar, times wuz 'ard backalong," she replied.

"An all backzevore," I added.

We enjoyed our walk down leafy lanes to Lamorna Cove with a stop at the pub on the way. The little harbour was perfect with the stream running onto the beach beside it. We set off westwards along the Coastal Path and soon found it hard work, climbing up and down on the cliffs, stopping to get our breath and gazing out to sea where little billows winked occasionally in the sun.

At one point Rosie slipped quite badly off the path. One of her legs went over the cliff and I had to stop myself deliberately pushing her into the wrinkled sea below. Instead I grabbed her arm and pulled her back safely onto the path somewhat shaken by my stupid urge. We walked on in silence ready to stop for lunch. Soon we came to a grassy field where daffodils were once grown and sat down in comfort to enjoy our lunch. We even had a short sleep on the warm turf with no dreams to spoil our day out. Rosie nearly trod on an adder which was basking in the sun and, once again, I guided her to safety while repressing the urge to grasp the snake and shake it in her face.

Self control is everything. It's a case of matter over mind and, as Rosie has done absolutely nothing to deserve the waves of hatred that come over me, she should not have to suffer the consequences of my strange obsessions.

We walked back to St Buryan along darkling lanes in the dimpsey. We both felt that we had thoroughly deserved our steaks and pints, Rosie for having walked so far and for having put up with a nervous and grumpy husband and me for having controlled myself.

That night the dream came back with a vengeance. I was back in the vault with the sound of waves crashing on a nearby shore and the light of the sea reflected from the ceiling of the tomb. Wilhelmina, although pale, showed none of the signs of death that she had previously exhibited. She beckoned to me and smiled from her coffin. I came to her and she sat up, wrapping her arms enthusiastically round me. They felt warm and quite normal. Her soft breath on my cheek was sweet and untainted.

Then she spoke. "Come back to me, dear

James. You'll always be mine. I don't know what I was doing when I left you."

Sunday 15th September

Waking up was harder than ever. But I managed it and even managed to be civil to Rosie. I felt that I could not go on like this, how could I choose between a live wife and a dead one? Clearly I needed help; when we went back home I would have to talk to Rosie and find some sort of therapy. Because I don't think I could carry on like this for long. Something would snap.

We decided to go to church at St Buryan. We walked up the steps past the ancient Celtic cross as the bells clashed in the tower. The vicar welcomed us at the door and we were shown to our pew by a sidesman. The organist played softly and well as we prepared ourselves for the service. The wind outside was getting up into a storm, rattling hard raindrops against the tall gothic windows of the church.

The vicar came in from the vestry and had to raise his voice against the rising wind. He asked us to pray for Tamsin Hoskins who had been killed on Friday in Penzance and especially for her family. A few muffled sobs came from the congregation and the service proceeded with the singing of the Gloria and the reading of the lessons.

The second lesson particularly interested me. It was about the casting out of devils from the boy who was possessed. Eventually the evil spirits were transferred to a heard of swine that were being kept for the Roman Army. The pigs stampeded in fear of their lives and all plunged off a cliff to their deaths. Once again, job done! The pigs, being unclean animals, would not have been missed by the Jewish people in the community. Only the Roman imperialists would have been upset and, well, they had it coming didn't they?

The sermon explained the reading and made a lot of sense to me. I had tried very hard not to behave like a swine but how long could I keep it up? Perhaps I could have a quiet word with the vicar after the service.

We went up to the altar rails to take communion and I experienced great difficulty in swallowing the wafer. The wine seemed to burn my lips. So I prayed hard for Rosie, for Wilhelmina, and for myself.

Feeling a little better I sat back in the pew to listen to the excellent organist play a voluntary after the service. Just before the priest went out to the vestry he explained that the piece of music chosen to remember Tamsin Hoskins was an unusual, even a controversial, choice. It had been her favourite piece of blues music. He had thought and prayed about it and had decided that the special arrangement of *Gloomy Sunday* could be played on the organ because it would not include the words. While he talked to us blasts of wind shook the lofty building.

We sat in a stunned silence as the spooky introduction descended abruptly to the swaying cadences that rose like a walk up the steps to the entrance of a dark crypt which loomed above. The descending cadences took me into the crypt where the inevitability of the draped coffin was no surprise. The last verse reminded me that it was all supposed to be a dream and that, despite the mood of the music, everything would turn out all right.

To me dreams had become more real than life itself. They had become objective because they were not controllable. Now I knew that I would not be able to talk to the vicar. In any case he probably had to hurry off to take the next service in one more of his scattered collection of parishes.

We walked quietly out of the church, our eyes on the floor. The muffled bells rank high above our heads.

"I do feel tired," Rosie told me. "I think I'll have a nap on the bed after lunch if you don't mind. The weather is too bad for a walk in any case."

"What a good idea. I'll take the car down to Lands End and have a look at the sea. I feel too restless to lie down."

We had an excellent lunch in the pub. Roast pork seemed somehow inappropriate after the church service but it was delicious. After coffee Rosie retired to bed and I felt a huge surge of annoyance and hatred. I tried not to let it show and I will always hope that I succeeded. I wished her good afternoon and walked across the windy car park to the car.

Switching on the wipers I turned on to what remained of the A30, now just a country lane leading to the end of the world. I drove carefully round the sharp bends past misty hills and crouching buildings. Soon the trees became stunted and bent and I passed the last pub and the last shop in Britain. I was running out of road and there was absolutely no going back.

The very end of the road consisted of a wind-buffeted gravel car park beyond a small unoccupied hut. Peering through the bleary windscreen I could just make out the humped hotel buildings and the attendant attractions, a wooden pirate ship, its naked spars stark against the troubled grey sky, and a dimly seen lifeboat squatting behind a stone wall.

I climbed out of the car. The gusting wind caught the door and rocked the car. Taking my diary and a pen I locked the car and walked across the puddled gravel expanse of the empty car park towards the dim buildings a few hundred yards away. Cloud fragments were blown across the chimneys of the hotel and I was rocked by the buffeting wind. My determination is complete; I want to save the life of the dear and innocent woman to whom I am married.

Now I'm level with the buildings but will not go in. Music blares from what appears to be a sideshow featuring pirates and half-naked wenches. The plaintive notes of *Gloomy Sunday* reach me on the wind, now near, now far away. I think grimly that I will never hear the song again.

On beyond the buildings towards the cliffs and the heaving Atlantic. Here is Ultima Thule. There is only one way to go from here....

[Here the diary ends. It was found on the turf at the top of the cliff in a soaking condition with the pen placed neatly beside it. There was no sign of Mr Thomas but his neatly-folded clothes were placed beside them.]

A witness, Miss Susan Tregenna, made this statement:

"I was looking out of the window of the hotel lounge wondering when the weather would lift so that I could walk back round the cliffs to Sennen. Suddenly I saw a naked man running towards the cliffs to the west of the hotel. He was heading straight for the lighthouse and running faster all the time. I rushed out of the French window shouting at him to stop. I am a nurse and so almost nothing shocks me. I hoped that I could reach him before he got to the cliff edge.

He was too far ahead of me and I saw him jump off the cliffs. Although I saw him fall my eyes were torn away by the sight of a glowing woman standing on a rock just above the angry surge of the waves. She seemed to float with both arms extended, her long hair blowing in the wind.

I never saw him hit the rocks or fall into the water. In my opinion I don't think his body will ever be found."

Statement from Mr Basil Semmens, landlord of the Hawkins Arms, St Buryan:

"When Mr Thomas had not come back from Lands End I went upstairs to check on Mrs Thomas. The bedroom door was unlocked so I knocked and went in. Mrs Thomas was lying on the bed with her mouth and eyes open. She was clearly dead so I immediately called the ambulance and she was taken away to Penzance."

Statement from Dr Ali Aziz, consultant at Penzance Hospital:

"Mrs Rose Thomas arrived at Casualty at 15.47 hours today, Sunday 15th September. She was dead on arrival and had died at least two hours previously. I examined her and found that she had died of sudden heart failure, a condition known years ago as 'died of fright'."

Statement from Detective Inspector Phil Pascoe:

"Regarding the death of Mrs Rose Thomas foul play is not suspected."

The Forces

At the point where the Dartmouth road turned towards the coast a smaller lane crossed it at an angle. A few houses lay on each side of the road and an old inn sat in the angle of the crossroads. Its swinging sign bore the unusual name 'The Forces' and in its dark bar were numerous wartime mementos harking back to the secret days of Operation Tiger.

The new landlord and his wife were soon to learn what Operation Tiger had been. Old Ern, one of the few regulars who made the long walk from Blackawton most evenings for his pints of ale, told Jim about the 'Amurikins' who came for nearly two years, throwing folk from their villages and farms to practise landing on the beach and fighting from field to field with live ammunition. They had done this, said Ern, so that they could throw 'they Germins' out of northern France and send them back to ''itler's Germinny'. A fair few were killed in the practices.

"Where were these soldiers buried?" asked Jim.

"I'd rather not tell 'ee," replied Ern. "'Tis better you should not know. You'll sleep better of a night. But one thing I can tell 'ee. The pub is now called 'The Forces' but 'twadden always so. This yer crossroads was once called 'Forches Cross' and 'twas 'ere that stood the gibbet where the hanged men hung in chains for a year and a day. Tarred black they were and they swung in the wind with a rattling of bones to discourage road agents and toby men. Made they boggers think twice it did to see 'em swinging against the sky and grinning down on 'em as if to say you carry on as you do an' you'll end up a hanging..."

Jim had never heard Ern go on like that and rather welcomed it. Trade had been rather slow since he and Jill took over the pub in the spring. It was a gloomy old place, lonely and full of rust and dust. So they decided to throw out all the old war relics and hang a few horse brasses on the mantelpiece. They bought some old pews and a couple of curved settles for the bar and tried to introduce an olde worlde atmosphere.

When summer came more people came to 'The Forces'. Some regretted the loss of the old American uniforms, helmets and burp guns, others liked the new look. The relics were stored safely in an outhouse beyond the car park awaiting the next auction at Ashburton. One relic remained, a rusty bayonet from a Garand Mk1 rifle that was stuck immovably in the oak mantelpiece above the grate. Neither Jim nor his friends could summon the strength to pull it out. It remained embedded in the dark grainy wood; someone with superhuman strength had rammed it in long ago, possibly in a blind fury.

One dark November night Jim was polishing glasses behind the bar. The wind blasted the walls of the building from all angles and the rain lashed down against the window panes. From time to time a solitary car swished by as the rough wind buffeted the inn.

Ern came in like a drowned rat and took off his old gabardine coat which hung dripping near the door.

"Pint of mild and bitter," he said absentmindedly.

"We have only mild and only bitter; the war's over you know," replied Jim in an amused tone.

"Quite right," said Ern. "I was too young for that in the war in any case. Make it a pint of Tribute then m'dear. Can't reckon what I was thinkin' of..."

"Quiet night," said Jim as a blast of wind shook the casement.

"I reckon there'll be a crowd in here in a minute. I saw a whole group of soldiers out in a field just now, them re-enactors I calls 'em. They'll be in 'ere for their mild and bitter avore long, you mark my words."

Against the steady swish of the rain Jim heard the clatter and scrape of boots just outside the door.

The door swung inwards and, caught by the wind, banged hard against the wall. A group of scruffy American soldiers slouched in, the straps of their pot helmets swinging against their stubbled cheeks. They were filthy, plastered in mud and sand and the unwashed smell of them assailed Jim's nostrils. One of them closed the door with a bang and, one by one, they dropped their helmets in a pile by the door. Their leader, a tall thin man with close cut blonde hair, came up to the bar and leaned wearily on the polished wood. The impressive stripes on his arm showed him to be a senior non-commissioned officer. Bright blue eyes shone from a seamed and filthy face. The sour stink of his body was hard to take but Jim was a polite man. He was also very interested in these obviously dedicated re-enactors who had been out in all weathers for days.

"What can I do you for, sir?" Jim asked.

"Nine pints of bitter, please barkeep," muttered the soldier, his foul breath washing over the bar.

"Right you are pardner," said Jim pulling the first pint of over a gallon of real ale. He placed nine foaming pints on the bar and took the note from the soldier's cracked and grimy hand.

"Excuse me sir, there must be a mistake..." said Jim looking at the torn ten shilling note in his hand.

"Gimme a break," replied the soldier through gritted teeth. "Isn't our limey money good enough for you guys?"

Blue eyes bored into Jim's as the soldier pulled a packet of Lucky Strikes from an inner pocket of his stained combat jacket, placed one between his lips and struck a match on his thumb nail.

"Don't you know that you can't do that in here?" Jim croaked through the blue smoke that stung his eyes.

One by one the eight other soldiers walked up to the bar and stood accusingly behind their sergeant.

"D'y need a little help here Van Nostrand?" croaked a small squat corporal. Almost absently Jim noticed a small round hole in his forehead. The group seemed to slowly rise from the floor to hover just above the bar, their faces becoming pale and thin. Jim dropped his gaze to Van Nostrand's filthy hand inches away on the bar. He saw the flesh drop from the bones of the fingers in a writhing green sloughing and dared no more to raise his head.

The wind blasted and the rain spattered the window panes. Jim's sick heart dropped further as a bony hand clasped his shoulder. He let out a yell as his heart fluttered against his ribs.

"'Tis all right, they'm gone now," said Ern, shakily letting go of Jim's shoulder.

Jim looked up at last fully expecting to see a skeletal soldier grinning into his face. He was relieved when he saw nobody at all in front of the bar. The foul stink of the men remained to show him that they had indeed been there.

"They were here weren't they?" asked Jim desperately.

"Oh yes, indeed they were, a small section of the legion of the damned. They comes in here every year on November 2nd, All Souls' Day. Now they're back in their graves in the field across the road. I'd hoped they would not be back, what with the change of landlord an all. They always leave their mark..."

Jim looked over to the oak mantelpiece opposite the bar. The stink was beginning to fade; but the bayonet was gone. Splintered wood marked the place where it had been but it was gone. A tarnished coin lay on the planked floor in front of the fireplace. Ern picked it up and handed it to Jim who stood shaking behind the bar.

"'Tis a dime, sure enough. Keep it here above the bar for safe keeping. Maybe none of they soldiers will be back to claim it," said Ern.

"Whatever next?" replied Jim in a small voice.

"That's sometimes a question better not asked," said Ern in a grim voice.

Both men, alone in the shadowy bar heard the tap of footsteps as the wind lulled for a moment. They also heard something dragging behind. Once more the door blew in with a flutter of wet leaves.

An unspeakably pathetic figure stood framed in

the doorway. The hanged man was skeletal and tarred black. His head lolled on one side, the idiot jaw grinning slackly. There was no life in the dull eyes as the man slowly raised his chained arms in a mute greeting that was horribly familiar to the two horror-struck men in the bar...

Afterword

Here we are at the end of another haunted journey through the south west with a quick trip to the mid west. The title of the book is taken from a sign at the entrance to a small hilltop cemetery in Orrville, Ohio. I love American graveyards and the signs put up to protect them. One of my favourites is found in the centre of Key West with a wonderfully misspelled sign which says: 'Cemetary Gates Close at Dusk'.

The first story 'Tiddly Suits in Guz' was written before I embarked on *All Cornwall Thunders at my Door*, my biography of the great Cornish poet Charles Causley who is mentioned under the name of Bartlett in this story. I wrote the story in complete ignorance of any connection between Causley and the sinking of HMS Hood apart from in my imagination. Another eerie coincidence was the name 'Frank'; Causley actually had a close friend named Frank while stationed in Gibraltar.

When the Hood was sunk Causley was a Royal Naval Coder based in Gibraltar rather than a sailor on shore leave in Plymouth. He received the news of the sinking while on watch and had the unenviable job of reporting the fact to his captain. The loss of almost all the crew and one of the navy's greatest ships affected him very deeply to the extent that some of his old friends still mention it today. In my story art did not imitate life, neither did life imitate art. I changed the young sailor's name to Bartlett in a feeble attempt to set the record straight.

This story was beautifully read on our local radio Soundart by Chris Waters who was the chairman of the committee that awarded me a prize a few years ago for my ghost story 'Mr Hendra's Charabanc'. By a strange coincidence both stories associated with Chris are the first stories in both *Westcountry Stories of the Restless Dead* and this collection.

'The 9.50 to Penzance' harks back to the worst accident in the whole history of the Great Western Railway. By a strange coincidence it was the second accident that occurred on the railway at Norton Fitzwarren, on the London to Penzance main line just west of Taunton. The same strange set of two accidents in exactly the same place also happened on the GWR at Doublebois in Cornwall.

The Norton Fitzwarren accident killed thirty people, including Fireman Seabridge whose body was dug out from under a pile of coal on the footplate. Driver Oakes had just been bombed out of his house in

London and had fatigue, foul weather and endless delays to deal with on his way to Taunton. He should not be judged too harshly for reading the wrong signal across a rain swept platform and accelerating the train away from a standing stop to disaster.

'Ellie and Mags' is the second story I have set at haunted and haunting Berry Pomeroy Castle near Totnes in Devon. I wrote it for my writer and publisher friend Bob Mann of Totnes whose publishing house Longmarsh Press has recently published a book of stories and poems based on Berry Pomeroy Castle entitled *A Most Haunting Castle*.

The mediaeval Pomeroy sisters Eleanor and Margaret had the misfortune to fall in love with the same man. Eleanor had her younger and prettier sister imprisoned in a round corner tower of the castle that is roofless today and known as the St Margaret Tower. There she died, pining for her lover and her lost freedom. There are well known stories of her wraith appearing over the centuries, usually with fatal results.

The phenomenon of the appearance of glass in the empty tower window has been noted by others as well as by me. I cannot explain it; before being told about it by other people I had seen it on two occasions.

Blessed Cuthbert Mayne in 'I shall be with you' was hanged, drawn and quartered for being a Catholic priest in 1577 when the protestant Queen Elizabeth was on the throne. He is known as a protomartyr in light of what happened to Catholic priests in future years. References to him crop up repeatedly in Launceston where he was killed; his skull is kept in a nearby monastery and venerated as a holy relic. His fate has much to tell us today about intolerance.

'Limehouse Lane' is a truly beastly story, the central image of which came to me in a very vivid dream a few years ago. Last year I was returning home on a night flight from Florida. As I sat in my cramped and uncomfortable seat somewhere above eastern Canada I wrote the story in my head and memorised it. Limehouse Lane is a lane that leads down to Bow Creek, a tributary of the River Dart, from my home village of Ashprington. I have enjoyed family picnics down the lane for most of my life. Thank heavens that I have never had occasion to stumble across human remains in the lane. My mother was convinced that one day she would find a dead person in a wood. She never did, but a distant cousin who was a keen swimmer found a corpse floating in the Thames and another dead body clutching an umbrella in the sea off Brighton. She never went swimming again.

Dreams are powerful allies to a writer of ghost stories. The story 'Major Wiley' sprang from a dream of the three images of the wartime photographs of the good, or otherwise, fictitious brother of the notorious Alistair Crowley. In my dream the images were in

212

colour which made waking up a great relief.

I love churchyards, graveyards and cemeteries. 'Return of the Native' (I apologise to the late Mr Hardy) is set in Ashprington. Last year I did dig up a number of subterranean gravestones much as described in the story. I did so with permission and set three of the stones upright in the churchyard. The research of the families on the stones was fascinating and provided some good material for the Parish Magazine.

The one story which is completely true in every detail is 'Silly Cat'. I wrote it with, for once, no apology. Every detail of my dream was clear and exact; I put it in the book with no comment. I only know that it happened just like that.

'The Old People' who turned out to be remarkably low church are another example of religious intolerance. The incident that inspired this nasty little story happened at South Brent in the Middle Ages when the unfortunate priest John Hay was dragged out of his church and murdered just after evensong. Such an event would probably not happen today. Even so some parts of South Brent and the nearby moorland village of Didworthy have a sinister atmosphere that I find hard to ignore.

I must apologise once again, this time to the late M.R. James for using his title *A School Story*. James was the greatest writer of ghost stories that I know of; *Lost Hearts* is probably his finest and was left out of the first edition of *Ghost Stories of an Antiquarian*. Its tight structure and efficient use of language make it a classic.

I used the village of Harberton as the setting for this chilling story which I wrote in the glacial depths of last winter. I changed a few details in the appearance of Pancho's monument and the family names for obvious reasons. Pancho was actually Tito who died at his boarding school at the age of ten in the 1890s. In reality the tragedy was compounded by no foul play.

Roughtor (pronounced Rowter), on Bodmin Moor, is the second highest point in Cornwall. Charlotte Dymond was murdered at Roughtor Ford on 14th April 1844 and her friend Matthew Weeks was hanged at Bodmin Jail for her murder. The illiterate farmhand was forced to sign a confession and was given no chance to plead in his own defence. I took the same line as the Cornish writer Jane Nancarrow in suspecting Thomas Prout of the murder. Her fine novel *Stones and Shadows* should become the last word on the subject.

Charles Causley's *Ballad of Charlotte Dymond* presents the majority view and does so memorably and beautifully. Perhaps we'll never really know who cut poor Charlotte's throat on that Sunday evening long ago.

I met a man in Launceston who lived in the farmhouse where Charlotte lived and worked. His son slept in the room that once was Charlotte's and the ghostly footsteps on the stairs leading to the room are often heard. There is no limping or dragging of a foot, so I rest my case.

On the first Tuesday of the month I go to a poetry evening at Shapham House near Ashprington. All the history in the story 'Poetry Evening' is true but Captain Pownoll has never to my knowledge returned to Sharpham for any reason. It must be one of the few grand country houses in England not to be haunted. Perhaps I will come across a ghost there one evening; but if a sighting is anticipated it generally doesn't happen. On the other hand when an apparition is not anticipated one may be pleasantly surprised...

The Kevin in the story is Kevin Pyne, the Dartmouth poet and river rat. He is a good friend and a fine poet whose poems come straight from the heart and are a treat both to read and to hear.

'The Signing' is just a bit of fun. I often drive over the Tamar to Jamaica Inn in the middle of Bodmin Moor to supply my friend Sean Mellor with books. In the number of book sales I compete with a dead woman. Daphne du Maurier vastly outsells me, but I keep trying.

Every summer I have the occasional dream of being a teacher again. This summer's turned out to be the nightmare entitled 'Parent Conference'. I could name the people in it but I won't; they happen to be alive and would not be as pleasant as their encrypted selves in the story. The dream image of the two coffins in the crypt will remain fresh in my memory for a very long time.

Ruth Manning-Saunders' wonderful book *The Witchcraft and Legends of Dartmoor* was published many years ago. I loved the story of 'Jan Coo' who was enticed one evening into the turbulent River Dart never to be seen again. So I combined the legend with another one about the Dart's voracious appetite for people and the result is the sinister story set near New Bridge, paradoxically Dartmoor's oldest bridge. Chris Waters recently read this story on Soundart Radio.

'The Bells of St Sylvanus' was written after a rather frustrating bell ringing day in east Cornwall. I have always felt that there is something remote and strange about the village of St Germans, particularly around the church. I would not be at all surprised by a materialisation somewhere in the vicinity on a future visit. I could not resist the ghastly pun at the end of the story and hope, once again, that I will be forgiven for it.

There is no such place as Bodmin, *Ohio* although I can see the mid-western town in my mind's eye. You will find people of Cornish extraction all over America and Canada especially in mining areas. My wife's grandparents emigrated from west Cornwall in 1912 and eventually settled in Ohio. Other members of the family followed and settled down to farm in north eastern Ohio. Unfortunately the train suicide did happen many years ago to a cousin.

The combination of trains and ghosts has been a fascinating one since Charles Dickens wrote his wonderfully chilling short story 'The Signalman'. The experience of researching a haunting that is happening to the researcher is compelling. Often the ghost guides you to the knowledge that will set him or her at rest; the coincidence of something in a dusty book forming the key to the mystery of a haunting is an amazing idea. A warning from beyond the grave could come straight to you from your local library.

How many Devonians remember Smokey Joe, the gentle Cornish tramp, who lived in a gateway beside Telegraph Hill until his death in 1975? I am not usually afraid of ghosts, but I seem to have a morbid fear of motorbikes. Ever since my student days I have had bad experiences with them. When I sold my last bike to a friend he proceeded to smash it up; his last comment on the matter was that you just can't take your eyes off the road for a minute!

'RAF Davidstow Moor' is an atmospheric mick take. My good friend and publisher Steve Darlow of Fighting High Publications is an enthusiastic cyclist and aficionado of deserted wartime airdromes. He has an encyclopaedic knowledge of all matters Bomber Command and knows the country round Ypres intimately. He also has a great sense of humour and so I will not apologise for killing him off.

My longest ghost story to date 'Lady Sings the Blues' was inspired by the monthly poetry group Poetry Conversations held at Sharpham House once a month. The last one was on the subject of gloom. When a lady played Billy Holiday's 1941 version of *Gloomy Sunday* I was struck by the haunting quality of the song and remembered reading about it years ago. In the dusty ghost section of my library I found a book that I had read back in 1983 that told the story of the song as I describe it in the story.

During my Fulbright Teaching Exchange year in southern California my family and I were haunted by the song *La Bamba* that seemed to be playing almost everywhere. It was originally recorded by Ritchie Valens who died in a light plane crash in the early '60s with Buddy Holly and the Big Bopper. Quite soon after the song was released again in 1987 Mrs Valenzuela, the mother of Ritchie Valens, died. After that the song was heard in every Pizza Hut, Burger King and Carl's Junior in the West.

Months later my family and I were sitting in a restaurant in Massachusetts, just south of Boston when I remarked that we hadn't heard *La Bamba* for a while. A second later we heard its familiar and frenzied rhythms once again. Nobody alive had overheard us because I had said it very quietly.

The arrival of the sudden idea to kill one's wife while quietly sitting in Truro Cathedral is quite one of the most chilling thoughts that I have had in a long time. I am glad to say that my wife is actually quite safe; she did, however, have nightmares after reading this story.

'Beati qui Durant' was written for my friends who run The Durant Arms in Ashprington. The first part about the female ghost floating about in the road is true; my wife and I were in the pub when the man arrived in a panic. There are psychic disturbances in The Durant Arms. The groaning sounds and flying glasses have actually happened.

I read in my local paper last week that the new barmaid at The Forces pub near Blackawton in south Devon served a customer who promptly vanished before her startled eyes. The story I then wrote was a bit of fun; the top sergeant Van Nostrand who died in the practice landings was a very distant cousin of mine. He came from New York and is buried near Cambridge. I have no idea who the hanged felon is, but I would hate to meet him in the pub on a dark night. It is quite possible that he also was a relative.

There are several indications that I should stop writing ghost stories. I am beginning to dream them and they are getting into my subconscious. It could be said that I am beginning to haunt myself. Such a thing is quite possible. The nineteenth century traveller Lady

Hester Stanhope spent a long time in Tibet where some of the people, by fasting and meditation, were able to create beings known as tulpas that began as thought forms and eventually took on an individual life of their own. After six months of prayer, fasting and other spiritual exercises Lady Hester created a crude lumpish creature that followed her everywhere and eventually had to be banished; at least that is what she claimed in her memoirs.

I am nowhere near to creating a tulpa, but I have met and talked with my own double. It happened in Dover, Ohio in 1974 at the famous Warther woodcarver's museum. My double was a gardener and the resemblance was uncanny; I even have a photograph to prove this point. If the man is still alive he will be nearing retirement and will know a lot more about gardening than I do.

My oldest son once saw his own image standing beside his bed in the middle of the night, an alarming experience.

In conclusion I will now take a break from writing ghost stories before I begin to frighten myself. The journey is over; it began three years ago with a story set in Cornworthy on All Souls' Day and ends with a story set near Blackawton on All Souls' Day. I will wish you au revoir, but not adieu.

Notes

These pages are for the reader to make notes about the stories or the locations visited.

Notes

Notes

About Laurence Green

Laurence Green is a retired teacher who has lived near Totnes in Devon nearly all his life. He is the author of the historical novel *A Hollow Sea: Thomas Prockter Ching and the Barque "Charles Eaton"*; the companion book of ghost stories *Westcountry Stories of the Restless Dead*, and a book on his grandfather *From Great War to Great Escape: The Two Wars of Fl Lieut Bernard 'Pop' Green MC*.

His biography of Charles Causley *All Cornwall Thunders at my Door* will be published in 2013. Future plans include a historical novel based on an ancestor, Capt. Thomas Carroll Shippen MD, who saved many lives during the American Civil War.

Laurence Green has written a number of magazine articles for *Family Tree, My Cornwall* and *An Baner Kernewek*. He has an MA in Anglo-American Literary Relations from the University of Exeter. His hobbies include battlefield exploration, railways, objets trouves, reading, research and dry stone walling.